The Positive School of Criminology

Enrico Ferri

Contents

THE POSITIVE SCHOOL OF CRIMINOLOGY

BY

Enrico Ferri

I.

My Friends:

When, in the turmoil of my daily occupation, I received an invitation, several months ago, from several hundred students of this famous university, to give them a brief summary, in short special lectures, of the principal and fundamental conclusions of criminal sociology, I gladly accepted, because this invitation fell in with two ideals of mine. These two ideals are stirring my heart and are the secret of my life. In the first place, this invitation chimed with the ideal of my personal life, namely, to diffuse and propagate among my brothers the scientific ideas, which my brain has accumulated, not through any merit of mine, but thanks to the lucky prize inherited from my mother in the lottery of life. And the second ideal which this invitation called up before my mind's vision was this: The ideal of young people of Italy, united in morals and intellectual pursuits, feeling in their social lives the glow of a great aim. It would matter little whether this aim would agree with my own ideas or be opposed to them, so long as it should be an ideal which would lift the aspirations of the young people out of the fatal grasp of egoistic interests. Of course, we positivists know very well, that the material requirements of life shape and determine also the moral and intellectual aims of human consciousness. But positive science declares the following to be the indispensable requirement for the regeneration of human ideals: Without an ideal, neither an individual nor a collectivity can live, without it humanity is dead or dying. For it is the fire of an ideal which renders the life of each one of us possible, useful and fertile. And only by its help can each one of us, in the more or less short course of his or her existence, leave behind traces for the benefit of fellow-beings. The invitation extended to me proves that the students of Naples believe in the inspiring existence of such an ideal of science, and are anxious to learn more about ideas, with which the entire world of the present day is occupied, and whose life-giving breath enters even through the windows of the dry courtrooms, when their doors are closed against it.

*   *   *   *   *

Let us now speak of this new science, which has become known in Italy by the name of the Positive School of Criminology. This science, the same as every other phenomenon of scientific evolution, cannot be shortsightedly or conceitedly attributed to the arbitrary initiative of this or that thinker, this or that scientist. We must rather regard it as a natural product, a necessary phenomenon, in the development of that sad and somber department of science which deals with the disease of crime. It is this plague of crime which forms such a gloomy and painful contrast with the splendor of present-day civilization. The 19th century has won a great victory over mortality and infectious diseases by means of the masterful progress of physiology and natural science. But while contagious diseases have gradually diminished, we see on the other hand that moral diseases are growing more numerous in our so-called civilization. While typhoid fever, smallpox, cholera and diphtheria retreated before the remedies which enlightened science applied by means of the experimental method, removing their concrete causes, we see on the other hand that insanity, suicide and crime, that painful trinity, are growing apace. And this makes it very evident that the science which is principally, if not exclusively, engaged in studying these phenomena of social disease, should feel the necessity of finding a more exact diagnosis of these moral diseases of society, in order to arrive at some effective and more humane remedy, which should more victoriously combat this somber trinity of insanity, suicide and crime.

The science of positive criminology arose in the last quarter of the 19th century, as a result of this strange contrast, which would be inexplicable, if we could not discover historical and scientific reasons for its existence. And it is indeed a strange contrast that Italy should have arrived at a perfect theoretical development of a classical school of criminology, while there persists, on the other hand, the disgraceful condition that criminality assumes dimensions never before observed in this country, so that the science of criminology cannot stem the tide of crime in high and low circles. It is for this reason, that the positive school of criminology arises out of the very nature of things, the same as every other line of science. It is based on the conditions of our daily life. It would indeed be conceited on our part to claim that we, who are the originators of this new science and its new conclusions, deserve alone the credit for its existence. The brain of the scientist is rather a sort of electrical accumulator, which feels and assimilates the vibrations and heart-beats of life, its splendor and its shame, and derives therefrom the conviction that it must of necessity provide for definite social wants. And on the other hand, it would be an evidence of intellectual short-sightedness on the part of the positivist man of science, if he did not recognize the historical accomplishments, which his predecessors on the field of science have left behind as indelible traces of their struggle against the unknown in that brilliant and irksome domain. For this reason, the adherents of the positive school of criminology feel the most sincere reverence for the classic school of criminology. And I am glad today, in accepting the invitation of the students of Naples, to say, that this is another reason why their invitation was welcome to me. It is now 16 years since I gave in this same hall a lecture on positive criminology, which was then in its initial stages. It was in 1885, when I had the opportunity to outline the first principles of the positive school of criminology, at the invitation of other students, who preceded you on the periodic waves of the intellectual generations. And the renewal of this opportunity gave me so much moral satisfaction that, I could not under any circumstances decline your invitation. Then too, the Neapolitan Atheneum has maintained the reputation of the Italian mind in the 19th century, also in that science which even foreign scientists admit to be our specialty, namely the science of criminology. In fact, aside from the two terrible books of the Digest, and from the practical criminologists of the Middle Ages who continued the study of criminality, the modern world opened a glorious page in the progress of criminal science with the modest little book of Cesare Beccaria. This progress leads from Cesare Beccaria, by way of Francesco Carrara, to Enrico Pessina.

Enrico Pessina alone remains of the two giants who concluded the cycle of classic school of criminology. In a lucid moment of his scientific consciousness, which soon reverted to the old abstract and metaphysical theories, he announced in an introductory statement in 1879, that criminal justice would have to rejuvenate itself in the pure bath of the natural sciences and substitute in place of abstraction the living and concrete study of facts. Naturally every scientist has his function and historical significance; and we cannot expect that a brain which has arrived at the end of its career should turn towards a new direction. At any rate, it is a significant fact that this most renowned representative of the classic school of criminology should have pointed out this need of his special science in this same university of Naples, one year after the inauguration of the positive school of criminology, that he should have looked forward to a time when the study of natural and positive facts would set to rights the old juridical abstractions. And there is still another precedent in the history of this university, which makes scientific propaganda at this place very agreeable for a positivist. It is that six years before that introductory statement by Pessina, Giovanni Bovio gave lectures at this university, which he published later on under the title of "A Critical Study of Criminal Law." Giovanni Bovio performed in this monograph the function of a critic, but the historical time of his thought, prevented him from taking part in the construction of a new science. However, he prepared the ground for new ideas, by pointing out all the rifts and weaknesses of the old building. Bovio maintained that which Gioberti, Ellero, Conforti, Tissol had already maintained, namely that it is impossible to solve the problem which is still the theoretical foundation of the classic school of criminology, the problem of the relation between punishment and crime. No man, no scientist, no legislator, no judge, has ever been able to indicate any absolute standard, which would enable us to say that equity demands a definite punishment for a definite crime. We can find some opportunistic expedient, but not a solution of the problem. Of course, if we could decide which is the gravest crime, then we could also decide on the heaviest sentence and formulate a descending scale which would establish the relative fitting proportions between crime and punishment. If it is agreed that patricide is the gravest crime, we meet out the heaviest sentence, death or imprisonment for life, and then we can agree on a descending scale of crime and on a parallel scale of punishments. But the problem begins right with the first stone of the structure, not with the succeeding steps. Which is the greatest penalty proportional to the crime of patricide? Neither science, nor legislation, nor moral consciousness, can offer an absolute standard. Some say: The greatest penalty is death. Others say: No, imprisonment for life. Still others say: Neither death, nor imprisonment for life, but only imprisonment for a time. And if imprisonment for a time is to be the highest penalty, how many years shall it last --thirty, or twenty-five, or ten?

No man can set up any absolute standard in this matter. Giovanni Bovio thus arrived at the conclusion that this internal contradiction in the science of criminology was the inevitable fate of human justice, and that this justice, struggling in the grasp of this internal contradiction, must turn to the civil law and ask for help in its weakness. The same thought had already been illumined by a ray from the bright mind of Filangieri, who died all too soon. And we can derive from this fact the historical rule that the most barbarian conditions of humanity show a prevalence of a criminal code which punishes without healing; and that the gradual progress of civilization will give rise to the opposite conception of healing without punishing.

Thus it happens that this university of Naples, in which the illustrious representative of the classic school of criminology realized the necessity of its regeneration, and in which Bovio foresaw its sterility, has younger teachers now who keep alive the fire of the positivist tendency in criminal science, such as Penta, Zuccarelli, and others, whom you know. Nevertheless I feel that this faculty of jurisprudence still lacks oxygen in the study of criminal law, because its thought is still influenced by the overwhelming authority of the name of Enrico Pessina. And it is easy to understand that there, where the majestic tree spreads out its branches towards the blue vault, the young plant feels deprived of light and air, while it might have grown strong and beautiful in another place.

The positive school of criminology, then, was born in our own Italy through the singular attraction of the Italian mind toward the study of criminology; and its birth is also due to the peculiar condition our country with its great and strange contrast between the theoretical doctrines and the painful fact of an ever increasing criminality.

The positive school of criminology was inaugurate by the work of Cesare Lombroso, in 1872. From 1872 to 1876 he opened a new way for the study of criminality by demonstrating in his own person that we must first understand the criminal who offends, before we can study and understand his crime. Lombroso studied the prisoners in the various penitentiaries of Italy from the point of view of anthropology. And he compiled his studies in the reports of the Lombardian Institute of Science and Literature, and published them later together in his work "Criminal Man." The first edition of this work (1876) remained almost unnoticed, either because its scientific material was meager, or because Cesare Lombroso had not yet drawn any general scientific conclusions, which could have attracted the attention of the world of science and law. But simultaneously with its second edition (1878) there appeared two monographs, which constituted the embryo of the new school, supplementing the anthropological studies of Lombroso with conclusions and systematizations from the point of view of sociology and law. Raffaele Garofalo published in the Neapolitan Journal of Philosophy and Literature an essay on criminality, in which he declared that the dangerousness of the criminal was the criterion by which society should measure the function of its defense against the disease of crime. And in the same year, 1878, I took occasion to publish a monograph on the denial of free will and personal responsibility, in which I declared frankly that from now on the science of crime and punishment must look for the fundamental facts of a science of social defense against crime in the human and social life itself. The simultaneous publication of these three monographs caused a stir. The teachers of classic criminology, who had taken kindly to the recommendations of Pessina and Ellero, urging them to study the natural sources of crime, met the new ideas with contempt, when the new methods made a determined and radical departure, and became not only the critics, but the zealous opponents of the new theories. And this is easy to understand. For the struggle for existence is an irresistible law of nature, as well for the thousands of germs scattered to the winds by the oak, as for the ideas which grow in the brain of man. But persecutions, calumnies, criticisms, and opposition are powerless against an idea, if it carries within itself the germ of truth. Moreover, we should look upon this phenomenon of a repugnance in the average intellect (whether of the ordinary man or the scientist) for all new ideas as a natural function. For when the brain of some man has felt the light of a new idea, a sneering criticism serves us a touchstone for it. If the idea is wrong, it will fall by the wayside; if it is right, then criticisms, opposition and persecution will cull the golden kernel from the unsightly shell, and the idea will march victoriously over everything and everybody. It is so in all walks of life--in art, in politics, in science. Every new idea will rouse against itself naturally and inevitably the opposition of the accustomed thoughts. This is so true, that when Cesare Beccaria opened the great historic cycle of the classic school of criminology, he was assaulted by the critics of his time with the same indictments which were brought against us a century later.

When Cesare Beccaria printed his book on crime and penalties in 1774 under a false date and place of publication, reflecting the aspirations which gave rise to the impending hurricane of the French revolution; when he hurled himself against all that was barbarian in the mediaeval laws and set loose a storm of enthusiasm among the encyclopedists, and even some of the members of government, in France, he was met by a wave of opposition, calumny and accusation on the part of the majority of jurists, judges and lights of philosophy. The abbe Jachinci published four volumes against Beccaria, calling him the destroyer of justice and morality, simply because he had combatted the tortures and the death penalty.

The tortures, which we incorrectly ascribe to the mental brutality of the judges of those times, were but a logical consequence of the contemporaneous theories. It was felt that in order to condemn a man, one must have the certainty of his guilty, and it was said that the best means of obtaining tins certainty, the queen of proofs, was the confession of the criminal. And if the criminal denied his guilt, it was necessary to have recourse to torture, in order to force him to a confession which he withheld from fear of the penalty. The torture soothed, so to say, the conscience of the judge, who was free to condemn as soon as he had obtained a confession. Cesare Beccaria rose with others against the torture. Thereupon the judges and jurists protested that penal justice would be impossible, because it could not get any information, since a man suspected of a crime would not confess his guilt voluntarily. Hence they accused Beccaria of being the protector of robbers and murderers, because he wanted to abolish the only means of compelling them to a confession, the torture. But Cesare Beccaria had on his side the magic power of truth. He was truly the electric accumulator of his time, who gathered from its atmosphere the presage of the coming revolution, the stirring of the human conscience. You can find a similar illustration in the works of Daquin in Savoy, of Pinel in France, and of Hach Take in England, who strove to bring about a revolution in the treatment of the insane. This episode interests us especially, because it is a perfect illustration of the way traveled by the positive school of criminology. The insane were likewise considered to blame for their insanity. At the dawn of the 19th century, the physician Hernroth still wrote that insanity was a moral sin of the insane, because "no one becomes insane, unless he forsakes the straight path of virtue and of the fear of the Lord."

And on this assumption the insane were locked up in horrible dungeons, loaded down with chains, tortured and beaten, for lo! their insanity was their own fault.

At that period, Pinel advanced the revolutionary idea that insanity was not a sin, but a disease like all other diseases. This idea is now a commonplace, but in his time it revolutionized the world. It seemed as though this innovation inaugurated by Pinel would overthrow the world and the foundations of society. Well, two years before the storming of the Bastile Pinel walked into the sanitarium of the Salpetriere and committed the brave act of freeing the insane of the chains that weighed them down. He demonstrated in practice that the insane, when freed of their chains, became quieter, instead of creating wild disorder and destruction. This great revolution of Pinel, Chiarugi, and others, changed the attitude of the public mind toward the insane. While formerly insanity had been regarded as a moral sin, the public conscience, thanks to the enlightening work of science, henceforth had to adapt itself to the truth that insanity is a disease like all others, that a man does not become insane because he wants to, but that he becomes insane through hereditary transmission and the influence of the environment in which he lives, being predisposed toward insanity and becoming insane under the pressure of circumstances.

The positive school of criminology accomplished the same revolution in the views concerning the treatment of criminals that the above named men of science accomplished for the treatment of the insane. The general opinion of classic criminalists and of the people at large is that crime involves a moral guilt, because it is due to the free will of the individual who leaves the path of virtue and chooses the path of crime, and therefore it must be suppressed by meeting it with a proportionate quantity of punishment. This is to this day the current conception of crime. And the illusion of a free human will (the only miraculous factor in the eternal ocean of cause and effect) leads to the assumption that one can choose freely between virtue and vice. How can you still believe in the existence of a free will, when modern psychology armed with all the instruments of positive modern research, denies that there is any free will and demonstrates that every act of a human being is the result of an interaction between the personality and the environment of man?

And how is it possible to cling to that obsolete idea of moral guilt, according to which every individual is supposed to have the free choice to abandon virtue and give himself up to crime? The positive school of criminology maintains, on the contrary, that it is not the criminal who wills; in order to be a criminal it is rather necessary that the individual should find himself permanently or transitorily in such personal, physical and moral conditions, and live in such an environment, which become for him a chain of cause and effect, externally and internally, that disposes him toward crime. This is our conclusion, which I anticipate, and it constitutes the vastly different and opposite method, which the positive school of criminology employs as compared to the leading principle of the classic school of criminal science.

In this method, this essential principle of the positive school of criminology, you will find another reason for the seemingly slow advance of this school. That is very natural. If you consider the great reform carried by the ideas of Cesare Beccaria into the criminal justice of the Middle Age, you will see that the great classic school represents but a small step forward, because it leaves the penal justice on the same theoretical and practical basis which it had in the Middle Age and in classic antiquity, that is to say, based on the idea of a moral responsibility of the individual. For Beccaria, for Carrara, for their predecessors, this idea is no more nor less than that mentioned in books 47 and 48 of the Digest: "The criminal is liable to punishment to the extent that he is morally guilty of the crime he has committed." The entire classic school is, therefore, nothing but a series of reforms. Capital punishment has been abolished in some countries, likewise torture, confiscation, corporal punishment. But nevertheless the immense scientific movement of the classic school has remained a mere reform.

It has continued in the 19th century to look upon crime in the same way that the Middle Age did: "Whoever commits murder or theft, is alone the absolute arbiter to decide whether he wants to commit the crime or not." This remains the foundation of the classic school of criminology. This explains why it could travel on its way more rapidly than the positive school of criminology. And yet, it took half a century from the time of Beccaria, before the penal codes showed signs of the reformatory influence of the classic school of criminology. So that it has also taken quite a long time to establish it so well that it became accepted by general consent, as it is today. The positive school of criminology was born in 1878, and although it does not stand for a mere reform of the methods of criminal justice, but for a complete and fundamental transformation of criminal justice itself, it has already gone quite a distance and made considerable conquests which begin to show in our country. It is a fact that the penal code now in force in this country represents a compromise, so far as the theory of personal responsibility is concerned, between the old theory of free will and the conclusions of the positive school which denies this free will.

You can find an illustration of this in the eloquent contortions of phantastic logic in the essays on the criminal code written by a great advocate of the classic school of criminology, Mario Pagano, this admirable type of a scientist and patriot, who does not lock himself up in the quiet egoism of his study, but feels the ideal of his time stirring within him and gives up his life to it. He has written three lines of a simple nudity that reveals much, in which he says: "A man is responsible for the crimes which he commits; if, in committing a crime, his will is half free, he is responsible to the extent of one-half; if one-third, he is responsible one-third." There you have the uncompromising and absolute classic theorem. But in the penal code of 1890, you will find that the famous article 45 intends to base the responsibility for a crime on the simple will, to the exclusion of the free will. However, the Italian judge has continued to base the exercise of penal justice on the supposed existence of the free will, and pretends not to know that the number of scientists denying the free will is growing. Now, how is it possible that so terrible an office as that of sentencing criminals retains its stability or vacillates, according to whether the first who denies the existence of a free will deprives this function of its foundation?

Truly, it is said that this question has been too difficult for the new Italian penal code. And, for this reason, it was thought best to base the responsibility for a crime on the idea that a man is guilty simply for the reason that he wanted to commit the crime; and that he is not responsible if he did not want to commit it. But this is an eclectic way out of the difficulty, which settles nothing, for in the same code we have the rule that involuntary criminals are also punished, so that involuntary killing and wounding are punished with imprisonment the same as voluntary deeds of this kind. We have heard it said in such cases that the result may not have been intended, but the action bringing it about was. If a hunter shoots through a hedge and kills or wounds a person, he did not intend to kill, and yet he is held responsible because his first act, the shooting, was voluntary.

That statement applies to involuntary crimes, which are committed by some positive act. But what about involuntary crimes of omission? In a railway station, where the movements of trains represent the daily whirl of traffic in men, things, and ideas, every switch is a delicate instrument which may cause a derailment. The railway management places a switchman on duty at this delicate post. But in a moment of fatigue, or because he had to work inhumanly long hours of work, which exhausted all his nervous elasticity, or for other reasons, the switchman forgets to set the switch and causes a railroad accident, in which people are killed and wounded. Can it be said that he intended the first act? Assuredly not, for he did not intend anything and did not do anything. The hunter who fires a shot has at least had the intention of shooting. But the switchman did not want to forget (for in that case he would be indirectly to blame); he has simply forgotten from sheer fatigue to do his duty; he has had no intention whatever, and yet you hold him responsible in spite of all that! The fundamental logic of your reasoning in this case corresponds to the logic of the things. Does it not happen every day in the administration of justice that the judges forget about the neutral expedient of the legislator who devised this relative progress of the penal code, which pretends to base the responsibility of a man on the neutral and naive criterion of a will without freedom of will? Do they not follow their old mental habits in the administration of justice and apply the obsolete criterion of the free will, which the legislator thought fit to abandon? We see, then, as a result of this imperfect and insincere innovation in penal legislation this flagrant contradiction, that the magistrates assume the existence of a free will, while the legislator has decided that it shall not be assumed. Now, in science as well as in legislation, we should follow a direct and logical line, such as that of the classic school or the positive school of criminology. But whoever thinks he has solved a problem when he gives us a solution which is neither fish nor fowl, comes to the most absurd and iniquitous conclusions. You see what happens every day. If to-morrow some beastly and incomprehensible crime is committed, the conscience of the judge is troubled by this question: Was the person who committed this crime morally free to act or not? He may also invoke the help of legislation, and he may take refuge in article 46,[A] or in that compromise of article 47,[B] which admits a responsibility of one-half or one-third, and he would decide on a penalty of one-half or one-third.

All this may take place in the case of a grave and strange crime. And on the other hand, go to the municipal courts or to the police courts, where the magic lantern of justice throws its rays upon the nameless human beings who have stolen a bundle of wood in a hard winter, or who have slapped some one in the face during a brawl in a saloon. And if they should find a defending lawyer who would demand the appointment of a medical expert, watch the reception he would get from the judge. When justice is surprised by a beastly and strange crime, it feels the entire foundation of its premises shaking, it halts for a moment, it calls in the help of legal medicine, and reflects before it sentences. But in the case of those poor nameless creatures, justice does not stop to consider whether that microbe in the criminal world who steals under the influence of hereditary or acquired degeneration, or in the delirium of chronic hunger, is not worthy of more pity. It rather replies with a mephistophelian grin when he begs for a humane understanding of his case.

[A] Article 46: "A person is not subject to punishment, if at the moment of his deed he was in a mental condition which deprived him of consciousness or of the freedom of action. But if the judge considers it dangerous to acquit the prisoner, he has to transfer him to the care of the proper authorities, who will take the necessary precautions."

[B] Article 47: "If the mental condition mentioned in the foregoing article was such as to considerably decrease the responsibility, without eliminating it entirely, the penalty fixed upon the crime committed is reduced according to the following rules:

"I. In place of penitentiary, imprisonment for not less than six years.

"II. In place of the permanent loss of civic rights, a loss of these rights for a stipulated time.

"III. Whenever it is a question of a penalty of more than twelve years, it is reduced to from three to ten years; if of more than six years, but not more than twelve, it is reduced to from one to five years; in other cases, the reduction is to be one-half of the ordinary penalty.

"IV. A fine is reduced to one-half.

"V. If the penalty would be a restriction of personal liberty, the judge may order the prisoner to a workhouse, until the proper authorities object, when the remainder of the sentence is carried out in the usual manner."

It is true that there is now and then in those halls of justice, which remain all too frequently closed to the living wave of public sentiment, some more intelligent and serene judge who is touched by this painful understanding of the actual human life. Then he may, under the illogical conditions of penal justice, with its compromise between the exactness of the classic and that of the positive school of criminology, seek for some expedient which may restore him to equanimity.

In 1832, France introduced a penal innovation, which seemed to represent an advance on the field of justice, but which is in reality a denial of justice: The expedient of ***extenuating circumstances***. The judge does not ask for the advice of the court physician in the case of some forlorn criminal, but condemns him without a word of rebuke to society for its complicity. But in order to assuage his own conscience he grants him extenuating circumstances, which seem a concession of justice, but are, in reality, a denial of justice. For you either believe that a man is responsible for his crime, and in that case the concession of extenuating circumstances is a hypocrisy; or you grant them in good faith, and then you admit that the man was in circumstances which reduced his moral responsibility, and thereby the extenuating circumstances become a denial of justice. For if your conviction concerning such circumstances were sincere, you would go to the bottom of them and examine with the light of your understanding all those innumerable conditions which contribute toward those extenuating circumstances. But what are those extenuating circumstances? Family conditions? Take it that a child is left alone by its parents, who are swallowed up in the whirl of modern industry, which overthrows the laws of nature and forbids the necessary rest, because steam engines do not get tired and day work must be followed by night work, so that the setting of the sun is no longer the signal for the laborer to rest, but to begin a new shift of work. Take it that this applies not alone to adults, but also to human beings in the growing stage, whose muscular power may yield some profit for the capitalists. Take it that even the mother, during the period of sacred maternity, becomes a cog in the machinery of industry. And you will understand that the child must grow up, left to its own resources, in the filth of life, and that its history will be inscribed in criminal statistics, which are the shame of our so-called civilization.

Of course, in this first lecture I cannot give you even a glimpse of the positive results of that modern science which has studied the criminal and his environment instead of his crimes. And I must, therefore, limit myself to a few hints concerning the historical origin of the positive school of criminology. I ought to tell you something concerning the question of free will. But you will understand that such a momentous question, which is worthy of a deep study of the many-sided physical, moral, intellectual life, cannot be summed up in a few short words. I can only say that the tendency of modern natural sciences, in physiology as well as psychology, has overruled the illusions of those who would fain persist in watching psychological phenomena merely within themselves and think that they can understand them without any other means. On the contrary, positive science, backed by the testimony of anthropology and of the study of the environment, has arrived at the following conclusions: The admission of a free will is out of the question. For if the free will is but an illusion of our internal being, it is not a real faculty possessed by the human mind. Free will would imply that the human will, confronted by the choice of making voluntarily a certain determination, has the last decisive word under the pressure of circumstances contending for and against this decision; that it is free to decide for or against a certain course independently of internal and external circumstances, which play upon it, according to the laws of cause and effect.

Take it that a man has insulted me. I leave the place in which I have been insulted, and with me goes the suggestion of forgiveness or of murder and vengeance. And then it is assumed that a man has his complete free will, unless he is influenced by circumstances explicitly enumerated by the law, such as minority, congenital deaf-muteness, insanity, habitual drunkenness and, to a certain extent, violent passion. If a man is not in a condition mentioned in this list, he is considered in possession of his free will, and if he murders he is held morally responsible and therefore punished.

This illusion of a free will has its source in our inner consciousness, and is due solely to the ignorance in which we find ourselves concerning the various motives and different external and internal conditions which press upon our mind at the moment of decision.

If a man knows the principal causes which determine a certain phenomenon, he says that this phenomenon is inevitable. If he does not know them, he considers it as an accident, and this corresponds in the physical field to the arbitrary phenomenon of the human will which does not know whether it shall decide this way or that. For instance, some of us were of the opinion, and many still are, that the coming and going of meteorological phenomena was accidental and could not he foreseen. But in the meantime, science has demonstrated that they are likewise subject to the law of causality, because it discovered the causes which enable us to foresee their course. Thus weather prognosis has made wonderful progress by the help of a network of telegraphically connected meteorological stations, which succeeded in demonstrating the connection between cause and effect in the case of hurricanes, as well as of any other physical phenomenon. It is evident that the idea of accident, applied to physical nature, is unscientific. Every physical phenomenon is the necessary effect of the causes that determined it beforehand. If those causes are known to us, we have the conviction that that phenomenon is necessary, is fate, and, if we do not know them, we think it is accidental. The same is true of human phenomena. But since we do not know the internal and external causes in the majority of cases, we pretend that they are free phenomena, that is to say, that they are not determined necessarily by their causes. Hence the spiritualistic conception of the free will implies that every human being, in spite of the fact that their internal and external conditions are necessarily predetermined, should be able to come to a deliberate decision by the mere fiat of his or her free will, so that, even though the sum of all the causes demands a no, he or she can decide in favor of yes, and vice versa. Now, who is there that thinks, when deliberating some action, what are the causes that determine his choice? We can justly say that the greater part of our actions are determined by habit, that we make up our minds almost from custom, without considering the reason for or against. When we get up in the morning we go about our customary business quite automatically, we perform it as a function in which we do not think of a free will. We think of that only in unusual and grave cases, when we are called upon to make some special choice, the so-called voluntary deliberation, and then we weigh the reasons for or against; we ponder, we hesitate what to do. Well, even in such cases, so little depends on our will in the deliberations which we are about to take that if any one were to ask us one minute before we have decided what we are going to do, we should not know what we were going to decide. So long as we are undecided, we cannot foresee what we are going to decide; for under the conditions in which we live that part of the psychic process takes place outside of our consciousness. And since we do not know its causes, we cannot tell what will be its effects. Only after we have come to a certain decision can we imagine that it was due to our voluntary action. But shortly before we could not tell, and that proves that it did not depend on us alone. Suppose, for instance, that you have decided to play a joke on a fellow-student, and that you carry it out. He takes it unkindly. You are surprised, because that is contrary to his habits and your expectations. But after a while you learn that your friend had received bad news from home on the preceding morning and was therefore not in a condition to feel like joking, and then you say: "If we had known that we should not have decided to spring the joke on him." That is equivalent to saying that, if the balance of your will had been inclined toward the deciding motive of no, you would have decided no; but not knowing that your friend was distressed and not in his habitual frame of mind, you decided in favor of yes. This sentence: "If I had known this I should not have done that" is an outcry of our internal consciousness, which denies the existence of a free will.

On the other hand, nothing is created and nothing destroyed either in matter or in force, because both matter and force are eternal and indestructible. They transform themselves in the most diversified manner, but not an atom is added or taken away, not one vibration more or less takes place. And so if is the force of external and internal circumstances which determines the decision of our will at any given moment. The idea of a free will, however, is a denial of the law of cause and effect, both in the field of philosophy and theology. Saint Augustine and Martin Luther furnish irrefutable theological arguments for the denial of a free will. The omnipotence of God is irreconcilable with the idea of free will. If everything that happens does so because a superhuman and omnipotent power wants it (Not a single leaf falls to the ground without the will of God), how can a son murder his father without the permission and will of God? For this reason Saint Augustine and Martin Luther have written ***de servo arbitrio***.

But since theological arguments serve only those who believe in the concept of a god, which is not given to us by science, we take recourse to the laws which we observe in force and matter, and to the law of causality. If modern science has discovered the universal link which connects all phenomena through cause and effect, which shows that every phenomenon is the result of causes which have preceded it; if this is the law of causality, which is at the very bottom of modern scientific thought, then it is evident that the admission of free thought is equivalent to an overthrow of this law, according to which every effect is proportionate to its cause. In that case, this law, which reigns supreme in the entire universe, would dissolve itself into naught at the feet of the human being, who would create effects with his free will not corresponding to their causes! It was all right to think so at a time when people had an entirely different idea of human beings. But the work of modern science, and its effect on practical life, has resulted in tracing the relations of each one of us with the world and with our fellow beings. And the influence of science may be seen in the elimination of great illusions which in former centuries swayed this or that part of civilized humanity. The scientific thought of Copernicus and Galilei did away with the illusions which led people to believe that the earth was the center of the universe and of creation.

Take Cicero's book *de Officiis*, or the *Divina Commedia* of Dante, and you will find that to them the earth is the center of creation, that the infinite stars circle around it, and that man is the king of animals: a geocentric and anthropocentric illusion inspired by immeasurable conceit. But Copernicus and Galilei came and demonstrated that the earth does not stand still, but that it is a grain of cosmic matter hurled into blue infinity and rotating since time unknown around its central body, the sun, which originated from an immense primitive nebula. Galilei was subjected to tortures by those who realized that this new theory struck down many a religious legend and many a moral creed. But Galilei had spoken the truth, and nowadays humanity no longer indulges in the illusion that the earth is the center of creation.

But men live on illusions and give way but reluctantly to the progress of science, in order to devote themselves arduously to the ideal of the new truths which rise out of the essence of things of which mankind is a part. After the geocentric illusion had been destroyed, the anthropocentric illusion still remained. On earth, man was still supposed to be king of creation, the center of terrestrial life. All Species of animals, plants and minerals were supposed to be created expressly for him, and to have had from time immemorial the forms which we see now, so that the fauna and flora living on our planet have always been what they are today. And Cicero, for instance, said that the heavens were placed around the earth and man in order that he might admire the beauty of the starry firmament at night, and that animals and plants were created for his use and pleasure. But in 1856 Charles Darwin came and, summarizing the results of studies that had been carried on for a century, destroyed in the name of science the superb illusion that man is the king and center of creation. He demonstrated, amid the attacks and calumnies of the lovers of darkness, that man is not the king of creation, but merely the last link of the zoological chain, that nature is endowed with eternal energies by which animal and plant life, the same as mineral life (for even in crystals the laws of life are at work), are transformed from the invisible microbe to the highest form, man.

The anthropocentric illusion rebelled against the word of Darwin, accusing him of lowering the human life to the level of the dirt or of the brute. But a disciple of Darwin gave the right answer, while propagating the Darwinian theory at the university of Jena. It was Haeckel, who concluded: "For my part, and so far as my human consciousness is concerned, I prefer to be an immensely perfected ape rather than to be a degenerated and debased Adam."

Gradually the anthropocentric illusion has been compelled to give way before the results of science, and today the theories of Darwin have become established among our ideas. But another illusion still remains, and science, working in the name of reality, will gradually eliminate it, namely the illusion that the nineteenth century has established a permanent order of society. While the geocentric and anthropocentric illusions have been dispelled, the illusion of the immobility and eternity of classes still persists. But it is well to remember that in Holland in the sixteenth century, in England in the seventeenth, in Europe since the revolution of 1789, we have seen that freedom of thought in science, literature and art, for which the bourgeoisie fought, triumphed over the tyranny of the mediaeval dogma. And this condition, instead of being a glorious but transitory stage, is supposed to be the end of the development of humanity, which is henceforth condemned not to perfect itself any more by further changes. This is the illusion which serves as a fundamental argument against the positive school of criminology, since it is claimed that a penal justice enthroned on the foundations of Beccaria and Carrara would be a revolutionary heresy. It is also this illusion which serves as an argument against those who draw the logical consequences in regard to the socialistic future of humanity, for the science which takes its departure front the work of Copernicus, Galilei and Darwin arrives logically at socialism. Socialism is but the natural and physical transformation of the economic and social institutions. Of course, so long as the geocentric and anthropocentric illusions dominate, it is natural that the lore of stability should impress itself upon science and life. How could this living atom, which the human being is, undertake to change that order of creation, which makes of the earth the center of the universe and of man the center of life? Not until science had introduced the conception of a natural formation and transformation, of the solar system, as well as of the fauna and flora, did the human mind grasp the idea that thought and action can transform the world.

For this reason we believe that the study of the criminal, and the logical consequences therefrom, will bring about the complete transformation of human justice, not only as a theory laid down in scientific books, but also as a practical function applied every day to that living and suffering portion of humanity which has fallen into crime. We have the undaunted faith that the work of scientific truth will transform penal justice into a simple function of preserving society from the disease of crime, divested of all relics of vengeance, hatred and punishment, which still survive in our day as living reminders of the barbarian stage. We still hear the "public vengeance" invoked against the criminal today, and justice has still for its symbol a sword, which it uses more than the scales. But a judge born of a woman cannot weigh the moral responsibility of one who has committed murder or theft. Not until the experimental and scientific method shall look for the causes of that dangerous malady, which we call crime, in the physical and psychic organism, and in the family and the environment, of the criminal, will justice guided by science discard the sword which now descends bloody upon those poor fellow-beings who have fallen victims to crime, and become a clinical function, whose prime object shall be to remove or lessen in society and individuals the causes which incite to crime. Then alone will justice refrain from wreaking vengeance, after a crime has been committed, with the shame of an execution or the absurdity of solitary confinement.

On the one hand, human life depends on the word of a judge, who may err in the case of capital punishment; and society cannot end the life of a man, unless the necessity of legitimate self-defense demands it. On the other hand, solitary confinement came in with the second current of the classic school of criminology, when at the same time, in which Beccaria promulgated his ideas, John Howard traveled all over Europe describing the unmentionable horrors of mass imprisonment, which became a center of infection for society at large. Then the classic school went to the other extreme of solitary confinement, after the model of America, whence we adopted the systems of Philadelphia and Harrisburg in the first half of the nineteenth century. Isolation for the night is also our demand, but we object to continuous solitary confinement by day and night. Pasquale Mancini called solitary confinement "a living grave," in order to reassure the timorous, when in the name of the classic school, whose valiant champion he was, he demanded in 1876 the abolition of capital punishment. Yet in his swan song he recognized that the future would belong to the positive school of criminology. And it is this "living grave" against which we protest. It cannot possibly be an act of human justice to bury a human being in a narrow cell, within four walls, to prevent this being from having any contact with social life, and to say to him at the end of his term: Now that your lungs are no longer accustomed to breathing the open air, now that your legs are no longer used to the rough roads, go, but take care not, to have a relapse, or your sentence will be twice as hard.

In reality, solitary confinement makes of a human being either a stupid creature, or a raving beast. And "s'io dico il vero, l'effeto nol nasconde"--if I speak the truth, the facts will also reveal it--for criminality increases and expands, honest people remain unprotected, and those who are struck by the law do not improve, but become ever more antisocial through the repeated relapses. And so we have that contrast which I mentioned in the beginning of my lecture, that the theoretical side of criminal science is so perfected, while criminal conditions are painfully in evidence. The inevitable conclusion is the necessity of a progressive transformation of the science of crime and punishment.

II.

W̶e saw yesterday in a short historical review that the classic cycle of the science of crime and punishment, originated by Cesare Beccaria more than a century ago, was followed in our country, some twenty years since, by the scientific movement of the positive school of criminology. Let us see today how this school studied the problem of criminality, reserving for tomorrow the discussion of the remedies proposal by this school for the disease of criminality.

When a crime is committed in some place, attracting public attention either through the atrocity of the case or the strangeness of the criminal deed--for instance, one that is not connected with bloodshed, but with intellectual fraud--there are at once two tendencies that make themselves felt in the public conscience. One of them, pervading the overwhelming majority of individual consciences, asks: How is this? What for? Why did that man commit such a crime? This question is asked by everybody and occupies mostly the attention of those who do not look upon the case from the point of view of criminology. On the other hand, those who occupy themselves with criminal law represent the other tendency, which manifests itself when acquainted with the news of this crime. This is a limited portion of the public conscience, which tries to study the problem from the standpoint of the technical jurist. The lawyers, the judges, the officials of the police, ask themselves: What is the name of the crime committed by that man under such circumstances? Must it be classed us murder or patricide, attempted or incompleted manslaughter, and, if directed against property, is it theft, or illegal appropriation, or fraud? And the entire apparatus of practical criminal justice forgets at once the first problem, which occupies the majority of the public conscience, the question of the causes that led to this crime, in order to devote itself exclusively to the technical side of the problem which constitutes the juridical anatomy of the inhuman and antisocial deed perpetrated by the criminal.

In these two tendencies you have a photographic reproduction of the two schools of criminology. The classic school, which looks upon the crime as a juridical problem, occupies itself with its name, its definition, its juridical analysis, leaves the personality of the criminal in the background and remembers it only so far as exceptional circumstances explicitly stated in the law books refer to it: whether he is a minor, a deaf-mute, whether it is a case of insanity, whether he was drunk at the time the crime was committed. Only in these strictly defined cases does the classic school occupy itself theoretically with the personality of the criminal. But ninety times in one hundred these exceptional circumstances do not exist or cannot be shown to exist, and penal justice limits itself to the technical definition of the fact. But when the case comes up in the criminal court, or before the jurors, practice demonstrates that there is seldom a discussion between the lawyers of the defense and the judges for the purpose of ascertaining the most exact definition of the fact, of determining whether it is a case of attempted or merely projected crime, of finding out whether there are any of the juridical elements defined in this or that article of the code. The judge is rather face to face with the problem of ascertaining why, under what conditions, for what reasons, the man has committed the crime. This is the supreme and simple human problem. But hitherto it has been left to a more or less perspicacious, more or less gifted, empiricism, and there have been no scientific standards, no methodical collection of facts, no observations and conclusions, save those of the positive school of criminology. This school alone makes an attempt to solve in every case of crime the problem of its natural origin, of the reasons and conditions that induced a man to commit such and such a crime.

For instance, about 3,000 cases of manslaughter are registered every year in Italy. Now, open any work inspired by the classic school of criminology, and ask the author why 3,000 men are the victims of manslaughter every year in Italy, and how it is that there are not sometimes only as many as, say, 300 cases, the number committed in England, which has nearly the same number of inhabitants as Italy; and how it is that there are not sometimes 300,000 such cases in Italy instead of 3,000?

It is useless to open any work of classical criminology for this purpose, for you will not find an answer to these questions in than. No one, from Beccaria to Carrara, has ever thought of this problem, and they could not have asked it, considering their point of departure and their method. In fact, the classic criminologists accept the phenomenon of criminality as an accomplished fact. They analyze it from the point of view of the technical jurist, without asking how this criminal fact may have been produced, and why it repeats itself in greater or smaller numbers from year to year, in every country. The theory of a free will, which is their foundation, excludes the possibility of this scientific question, for according to it the crime is the product of the fiat of the human will. And if that is admitted as a fact, there is nothing left to account for. The manslaughter was committed, because the criminal wanted to commit it; and that is all there is to it. Once the theory of a free will is accepted as a fact, the deed depends on the fiat, the voluntary determination, of the criminal, and all is said.

But if, on the other hand, the positive school of criminology denies, on the ground of researches in scientific physiological psychology, that the human will is free and does not admit that one is a criminal because he wants to be, but declares that a man commits this or that crime only when he lives in definitely determined conditions of personality and environment which induce him necessarily to act in a certain way, then alone does the problem of the origin of criminality begin to be submitted to a preliminary analysis, and then alone does criminal law step out of the narrow and arid limits of technical jurisprudence and become a true social and human science in the highest and noblest meaning of the word. It is vain to insist with such stubbornness as that of the classic school of criminology on juristic formulas by which the distinction between illegal appropriation and theft, between fraud and other forms of crime against property, and so forth, is determined, when this method does not give to society one single word which would throw light upon the reasons that make a man a criminal and upon the efficacious remedy by which society could protect itself against criminality.

It is true that the classic school of criminology has likewise its remedy against crime--namely, punishment. But this is the only remedy of that school, and in all the legislation inspired by the theories of that school in all the countries of the civilized world there is no other remedy against crime but repression.

But Bentham has said: Every time that punishment is inflicted it proves its inefficacy, for it did not prevent the committal of that crime. Therefore, this remedy is worthless. And a deeper study of the cause of crime demonstrates that if a man does not commit a certain crime, this is due to entirely different reasons, than a fear of the penalty, very strong and fundamental reasons which are not to be found in the threats of legislators. These threats, if nevertheless carried out by police and prison keepers, run counter to those conditions. A man who intends to commit a crime, or who is carried away by a violent passion, by a psychological hurricane which drowns his moral sense, is not checked by threats of punishment, because the volcanic eruption of passion prevents him from reflecting. Or he may decide to commit a crime after due premeditation and preparation, and in that case the penalty is powerless to check him, because he hopes to escape with impunity. All criminals will tell you unanimously that the only thing which impelled them when they were deliberating a crime was the expectation that they would go scot free. If they had but the least suspicion that they might be detected and punished they would not have committed the crime. The only exception is the case in which a crime is the result of a mental explosion caused by a violent outburst of passion. And if you wish to have a very convincing illustration of the psychological inefficacy of legal threats, you have but to think of that curious crime which has now assumed a frequency never known to former centuries, namely the making of counterfeit money. For since paper money--from want or for reasons of expediency--has become a substitute of metal coin in the civilized countries, the making of counterfeit paper money has become very frequent in the nineteenth century. Now a counterfeiter, in committing his crime, must compel his mind to imitate closely the inscription of the bill, letter for letter, including that threatening passage, which says: *"The law punishes counterfeiting* ..." etc. Can you see before your mind's eye a counterfeiter, in the act of engraving on the stone or the others may ignore the penalty that awaits them, but he cannot. This illustration is convincing, for in cases of other crimes one may always assume that the criminal acted without thinking of the future, even when he was not in a transport of passion. But in the case of the counterfeiter the very act of committing the crime reminds him of the threat of the law, and yet he is imperturbable while perpetrating it.

Crime has its natural causes, which lie outside of that mathematical point called the free will of the criminal. Aside from being a juridical phenomenon, which it would be well to examine by itself, every crime is above all a natural and social phenomenon, and should be studied primarily as such. We need not go through so hard a course of study merely for the purpose of walking over the razor edge of juristic definitions and to find out, for instance, that from the time Romagnosi made a distinction between incompleted and attempted crime rivers of ink have been spilled in the attempt to find the distinguishing elements of these two degrees of crime. And finally, when the German legislator concluded to make no distinction between incompleted and attempted crime and to recognize only the completed crime in his code of 1871, we witnessed the spectacle of Carrara praising that legislator for leaving that subtile distinction out of his code. A strange conclusion on the part of a science, which cudgels its brains for a century to find the marks of distinction between attempted and incompleted crime, and then praises the legislator for ignoring it. And another classic jurist, Buccellati, proposed to do away with the theory of attempted crime by simply defining it as a crime by itself, or as--a violation of police laws! A science which comes to such conclusions is a science which moves in metaphysical abstractions, and we shall see that all these finespun questions which abound in classical science lose all practical value before the necessity of saving society from the plague of crime.

The method which we, on the other hand, have inaugurated is the following: Before we study crime from the point of view of a juristic phenomenon, we must study the causes to which the annual recurrence of crimes in all countries is due. These are natural causes, which I have classified under the three heads of anthropological, telluric and social. Every crime, from the smallest to the most atrocious, is the result of the interaction of these three causes, the anthropological condition of the criminal, the telluric environment in which he is living, and the social environment in which he is born, living and operating. It is a vain beginning to separate the meshes of this net of criminality. There are still those who would maintain the one-sided standpoint that the origin of crime may be traced to only one of these elements, for instance, to the social element alone. So far as I am concerned, I have combatted this opinion from the very inauguration of the positive school of criminology, and I combat it today. It is certainly easy enough to think that the entire origin of all crime is due to the unfavorable social conditions in which the criminal lives. But an objective, methodical, observation demonstrates that social conditions alone do not suffice to explain the origin of criminality, although it is true that the prevalence of the influence of social conditions is an incontestable fact in the case of the greater number of crimes, especially of the lesser ones. But there are crimes which cannot be explained by the influence of social conditions alone. If you regard the general condition of misery as the sole source of criminality, then you cannot get around the difficulty that out of one thousand individuals living in misery from the day of their birth to that of their death only one hundred or two hundred become criminals, while the other nine hundred or eight hundred either sink into biological weakness, or become harmless maniacs, or commit suicide without perpetrating any crime. If poverty were the sole determining cause, one thousand out of one thousand poor ought to become criminals. If only two hundred become criminals, while one hundred commit suicide, one hundred end as maniacs, and the other six hundred remain honest in their social condition, then poverty alone is not sufficient to explain criminality. We must add the anthropological and telluric factor. Only by means of these three elements of natural influence can criminality be explained. Of course, the influence of either the anthropological or telluric or social element varies from case to case. If you have a case of simple theft, you may have a far greater influence of the social factor than of the anthropological factor. On the other hand, if you have a case of murder, the anthropological element will have a far greater influence than the social. And so on in every case of crime, and every individual that you will have to judge on the bench of the criminal.

The anthropological factor. It is precisely here that the genius of Cesare Lombroso established a new science, because in his search after the causes of crime he studied the anthropological condition of the criminal. This condition concerns not only the organic and anatomical constitution, but also the psychological, it represents the organic and psychological personality of the criminal. Every one of us inherits at birth, and personifies in life, a certain organic and psychological combination. This constitutes the individual factor of human activity, which either remains normal through life, or becomes criminal or insane. The anthropological factor, then, must not be restricted, as some laymen would restrict it, to the study of the form of the skull or the bones of the criminal. Lombroso had to begin his studies with the anatomical conditions of the criminal, because the skulls may be studied most easily in the museums. But he continued by also studying the brain and the other physiological conditions of the individual, the state of sensibility, and the circulation of matter. And this entire series of studies is but a necessary scientific introduction to the study of the psychology of the criminal, which is precisely the one problem that is of direct and immediate importance. It is this problem which the lawyer and the public prosecutor should solve before discussing the juridical aspect of any crime, for this reveals the causes which induced the criminal to commit a crime. At present there is no methodical standard for a psychological investigation, although such an investigation was introduced into the scope of classic penal law. But for this reason the results of the positive school penetrate into the lecture rooms of the universities of jurisprudence, whenever a law is required for the judicial arraignment of the criminal as a living and feeling human being. And even though the positive school is not mentioned, all profess to be studying the material furnished by it, for instance, its analyses of the sentiments of the criminal, his moral sense, his behavior before, during and after the criminal act, the presence of remorse which people, judging the criminal after their own feelings, always suppose the criminal to feel, while, in fact, it is seldom present. This is the anthropological factor, which may assume a pathological form, in which case articles 46 and 47 of the penal code remember that there is such a thing as the personality of the criminal. However, aside from insanity, there are thousands of other organic and psychological conditions of the personality of criminals, which a judge might perhaps lump together under the name of extenuating circumstances, but which science desires to have thoroughly investigated. This is not done today, and for this reason the idea of extenuating circumstances constitutes a denial of justice.

This same anthropological factor also includes that which each one of us has: the race character. Nowadays the influence of race on the destinies of peoples and persons is much discussed in sociology, and there are one-sided schools that pretend to solve the problems of history and society by means of that racial influence alone, to which they attribute an absolute importance. But while there are some who maintain that the history of peoples is nothing but the exclusive product of racial character, there are others who insist that the social conditions of peoples and individuals are alone determining. The one is as much a one-sided and incomplete theory as the other. The study of collective society or of the single individual has resulted in the understanding that the life of society and of the individual is always the product of the inextricable net of the anthropological, telluric and social elements. Hence the influence of the race cannot be ignored in the study of nations and personalities, although it is not the exclusive factor which would suffice to explain the criminality of a nation or an individual. Study, for instance, manslaughter in Italy, and, although you will find it difficult to isolate one of the factors of criminality from the network of the other circumstances and conditions that produce it, yet there are such eloquent instances of the influence of racial character, that it would be like denying the existence of daylight if one tried to ignore the influence of the ethnical factor on criminality.

In Italy there are two currents of criminality, two tendencies which are almost diametrically opposed to one another. The crimes due to hot blood and muscle grow in intensity from northern to southern Italy, while the crimes against property increase from south to north. In northern Italy, where movable property is more developed, the crime of theft assumes a greater intensity, while crimes due to conditions of the blood are decreasing on account of the lesser poverty and the resulting lesser degeneration of the people. In the south, on the other hand, crimes against property are less frequent and crimes of blood more frequent. Still there also are in southern Italy certain cases where criminality of the blood is less frequent, and you cannot explain this in any other way than by the influence of racial character. If you take a geographical map of manslaughter in Italy, you will see that from the minimum, from Lombardy, Piedmont, and Venice, the intensity increases until it reaches its maximum in the insular and peninsular extreme of the south. But even there you will find certain cases in which manslaughter shows a lesser intensity.

For instance, the province of Benevent is surrounded by other provinces which show a maximum of crimes due to conditions of blood, while it registers a smaller number. Naples, again, shows a considerably smaller number of such cases than the provinces surrounding it, but it has a greater number of unpremeditated cases of manslaughter. Messina, Catania and Syracuse have a remarkably smaller number of blood crimes than Trapani, Girgenti and Palermo. It has been attempted to claim that this difference in criminality is due to social condition's, because the agricultural conditions in eastern Sicily are less degrading than those of Girgenti and Trapani, where the sulphur mines compel the miners to live miserably. But we should like to ask the following question in opposition to this idea: Why and in what respect are the agricultural conditions in some provinces better than in others? This condition is merely itself a result, not a cause of the first degree.

Since the theory of historical materialism, which I prefer to call economic determinism, has demonstrated that political, moral and intellectual phenomena are reactions on the economic conditions of any time and place, the attempt has been made to interpret this theory very narrowly and to pretend that the economic condition of a nation is a primary cause and not determined by any other. For my part, ever since I have demonstrated the perfect accord between the Marxian and the Darwinian theories, I have said: Very well, the economic conditions of a nation explain its political, moral, intellectual conditions, but the economic condition is in its turn the result of other factors. For instance, how can the industrialism of England in the nineteenth century be explained? Take away the coal mines (the telluric environment), and you could not have the economic conditions of England as they are. For the economic conditions are a result of favorable or unfavorable telluric conditions which are acted upon by the intelligence and energy of a certain race. Catania, Messina, Syracuse, are in a better economic condition, because they have better geographical conditions and a different race (of Grecian blood) than the other Sicilian provinces. So it is in Apulia and Naples, which have likewise a considerable mixture of Grecian blood. The northern tourists are still attracted by our art and visit the ruins of Taormina or Pesto, which are the relics of the Grecian race. And it is the Grecian blood which explains the lesser frequency of bloody crimes in those provinces. This is therefore evidently the influence of the race. And I maintain that the same fact is due in the province of Benevent to the admixture of Langobardian blood. For the Duchy of Benevent has had an influx of Langobardian elements since the seventh century. And as we know that the German and Anglo-Saxon race has the smallest tendency towards bloody crimes, the beneficial influence of this racial character in Benevent explains itself. On the other hand, there is much Saracen blood in the western and southern provinces of Sicily, and this explains the greater number of bloody crimes there. It is evident that the organic character of the inhabitants of that island, where you may still see the brutal and barbarian features of the Saracen by the side of those of the blond, cool and quiet Norman, contains a transfusion of the blood of diverse races. But it is also true that wherever a certain race has been predominant, there its influence is left behind in the individual and collective life.

Let this be enough so far as the anthropological factor of criminality is concerned. There are, furthermore, the telluric factors, that is to say, the physical environment in which we live and to which we pay no attention. It requires much philosophy, said Rousseau, to note the things with which we are in daily contact, because the habitual influence of a thing makes it more difficult to be aware of it. This applies also to the immediate influence of the physical conditions on human morality, notwithstanding the spiritualist prejudices which still weigh upon our daily lives. For instance, if it is claimed in the name of supernaturalism and psychism that a man is unhappy because he is vicious, it is equivalent to making a one-sided statement. For it is just as true to say that a man becomes vicious because he is unhappy. Want is the strongest poison for the human body and soul. It is the fountain head of all inhuman and antisocial feeling. Where want spreads out its wings, there the sentiments of love, of affection, of brotherhood, are impossible.

Take a look at the figures of the peasant in the far-off arid Campagna, the little government employee, the laborer, the little shop-keeper. When work is assured, when living is certain, though poor, then want, cruel want, is in the distance, and every good sentiment can germinate and develop in the human heart. The family then lives in a favorable environment, the parents agree, the children are affectionate. And when the laborer, a bronzed statue of humanity, returns from, his smoky shop and meets his white-haired mother, the embodiment of half a century of immaculate virtue and heroic sacrifices, then he can, tired, but assured of his daily bread, give room to feelings of affection, and he will cordially invite his mother to share his frugal meal. But let the same man, in the same environment, be haunted by the spectre of want and lack of employment, and you will see the moral atmosphere in his family changing as from day into night. There is no work, and the laborer comes home without any wages. The wife, who does not know how to feed the children, reproaches her husband with the suffering of his family. The man, having been turned away from the doors of ten offices, feels his dignity as an honest laborer assailed in the very bosom of his own family, because he has vainly asked society for honest employment. And the bonds of affection and union are loosened in that family. Its members no longer agree. There are too many children, and when the poor old mother approaches her son, she reads in his dark and agitated mien the lack of tenderness and feels in her mother heart that her boy, poisoned by the spectre of want, is perhaps casting evil looks at her and harboring the unfilial thought: "Better an open grave in the cemetery than one mouth more to feed at home!"

It is true, that want alone is not sufficient to prepare the soil in the environment of that suffering family for the roots of real crime and to develop it. Want will weaken the love and mutual respect among the members of that family, but it will not be strong enough alone to arm the hands of the man for a matricidal deed, unless he should get into a pathological mental condition, which is very exceptional and rare. But the conclusions of the positive school are confirmed in this case as in any other. In order that crime may develop, it is necessary that anthropological, social and telluric factors should act together.

We generally forget the conditions of the physical environment in which we live, because supernatural prejudice tells us that the body is a beast which we must forget in order to elevate ourselves into a spiritual life. Manzoni could designate the Middle Ages by the term "dirty." because they neglected the demands of elementary hygiene, and thus of human morality. For where the requirements of our physical body are neglected or offended, there no flower can bloom. The telluric environment has a great influence on our physical activity, by way of our nervous system. We feel differently disposed, according to whether a south or a north wind blows. When Garibaldi was on the Pampas, he observed that his companions were irascible and prone to violent quarrels, when the Pampero blew, and that their behavior changed, when this wind ceased. The great founders of criminal statistics, Quetelet and Guerry, observed that the change of seasons carried with it a change in criminality. Sexual crimes are less frequent in winter than in spring and summer. And with reference to this point I have maintained, and still maintain, that it is due to the combined effects of temperature and social conditions, if crimes against property increase in winter. For lack of employment, the want of food and shelter, intensify the misery and lead to attacks on property. On the other hand, the cold by itself reduces sexual crimes and personal assaults. And those who claim that the longer intercourse between people in summer time has also a social influence, are also partly in the right.

The most eloquent fact in this respect was mentioned by Murro, when he pointed out that this change in the frequency of bloody crimes, greater in the warm months than in winter, applied also to prisoners. Statistics show that breach of discipline is most frequent in hot seasons. The social factor does not enter there, because the social life is there the same in winter and in summer. This is, therefore, a practical proof of the influence of climate, and it is re-enforced by the fact that delirium and epilepsy in insane asylums are also more frequent in hot than in cold months. The influence of the telluric factors, then, cannot be denied, and the influence of the social factor intensifies it, as I have already shown by its most drastic and characteristic example, that of want. One can, therefore, understand that a man, whose morality has been shaken by the pressure of increasing want, may be led to commit a crime against property or persons.

It is certainly quite evident, that economic misery has an undeniable influence on criminality. And if you consider, that about 300,000 criminals are sentenced in Italy every year, 180,000 of them for minor crimes, and 120,000 for crimes which belong to the gravest class, you can easily see that the greater part of them due mainly to social conditions, for which it should not be so very difficult to find a remedy. The work of the legislator may be slow, difficult, and inadequate, so far as the telluric and anthropological factors are concerned. But it could surely be rapid, efficacious and prompt, so far as the social factors influencing criminality are concerned.

We have now demonstrated that crime has its natural source in the combined interaction of three classes of causes, the anthropological (organic and psychological) factor, the telluric factor, and the social factor. And by this last factor we must not only mean want, but any other condition of administrative instability in political, moral, and intellectual life. Every social condition which makes the life of man in society insincere and imperfect is a social factor contributing towards criminality. The economic factor is in evidence in our civilization wherever the law of free competition, which is but a form of disguised cannibalism, establishes the rule: *Your death is my life*. The competition of laborers for a limited number of places is equivalent to saying that those who secure a living do so at the expense of those who do not. And this is a disguised form of cannibalism. While it does not devour the competitor as primitive mankind did, it paralyzes him by calumnies, recommendations, protection, money, which, secure the place for the best bargainer and leave the most honest, talented, and self-respecting to the pangs of starvation.

Moreover, the economic factor exerts its crime-breeding influence also under the form of a superabundance of wealth. Indeed, in our present society, which is in the downward stage of transition from glorious bourgeois civilization, which constituted a golden page of human history in the 19th century, wealth itself is a source of crime. For the rich, who do not enjoy the advantage of manual or intellectual work, suffer from the corruption of leisure and vice. Gambling throws them into an unhealthy fever; the struggle and race for money poison their daily lives. And although the rich may keep out of reach of the penal code, still they have condemned themselves to a life devoted to hypocritical ceremonies, which are devoid of moral sentiment. And this life leads them to a sportive form of criminality. To cheat at gambling is the inevitable fate of these parasites. In order to kill time they give themselves up to games of chance, and those who do not care for that devote themselves to the sport of adultery, which in that class is a pastime even among the best friends, on account of sheer mental poverty. And all because man's mind unoccupied is the devil's own forge, as the English poet says.

We have now surveyed briefly the natural genesis of crime, as a natural social phenomenon, brought about by the interaction of anthropological, telluric, and social influences, which in any determined moment act upon a personality standing on the cross road of vice and virtue, crime and honesty. This scientific deduction gives rise to a series of investigations which satisfy the mind and supply it with a real understanding of things, far better than the theory that a man is a criminal because he wants to be. No, a man commits crime because he finds himself in certain physical and social conditions, from which the evil plant of crime takes life and strength. Thus we obtain the origin of that sad human figure which is the product of the interaction of those factors, an abnormal man, a man not adapted to the conditions of the social environment in which he is born, so that emigration becomes an ever more permanent phenomenon for the greater portion of men, for whom the accident of birth will less and less determine the course of their future life. And the abnormal man who is below the minimum of adaptability to social life and bears the marks of organic degeneration, develops either a passive or an aggressive form of abnormality and becomes a criminal.

Among these abnormal human beings, two groups must be particularly distinguished. Limiting our observations to those who are true aggressively antisocial abnormals, that is to say, who are not adapted to a certain social order and attack it by crimes, we must distinguish those who for egoistic or ferocious reasons attack society by atavistic forms of the struggle for existence by committing socalled common crimes in the shape of fraud or violence, thereby opposing or abolishing conditions in which their fellow beings may live. This is the atavistic type of criminals which represents an involutionary, or retrogressive, form of abnormality, due to an arrested development or an atavistic reversion to a savage and primitive type. These constitute the majority in the world of criminals and must be distinguished from the minority, who are evolutionary, or progressive, abnormals, that may also commit crime in a violent form, but must not be confounded with the others, because they do not act from egoistic motives, but rebel from altruistic motives against the injustice of the present order. These altruistic criminals feel the sufferings and horrors due to the injustice surrounding them and may go so far as to commit murder, which must always be condemned, but which must not be confounded with atavistic or egoistic murder. Recourse to personal violence is always objectionable from the point of view of higher manhood, which desires that human life should always be held in respect. But the reasons for such a crime are different, being egoistic in the one, and altruistic in the other case. The evolutionary abnormal is often an instrument of human progress, not in the form of criminality, but in that of intellectual and moral rebellion against conditions which are sanctioned by laws that frequently punish such an evolutionary rebellion harder than atavistic crime, as they do in Russia, where capital punishment has been abolished for common crimes, but retained for political violations of the law! We are living in an epoch of transition from the old to the new, and contemporaneous humanity has an uneasy moral conscience in this critical time. The ruling classes are losing their clearness of vision, so that they promise monuments to those political murderers who promoted their own historical victories, but would condemn like any common criminal him who now devotes his soul to a revolutionary ideal, would throw into prison the pioneer of new human ideals, just as Russia is excommunicating the rebel Tolstoi. I mention Leo Tolstoi advisedly for the purpose of giving a precise illustration of my heterodox thought in reference to this question. We are opposed to any form of personal violence (with the sole exception of self-defense), we cannot approve of any form of personal assault, no matter what may be its motive. Therefore we cannot have words of praise or excuse for political murder, though it may be inspired by altruistic motives. We can demand that the legislator should distinguish between the psychological sources of these two forms of murder, the egoistic and the altruistic form. But we condemn them both, because they are inhuman forms of violence. Ideas do not make victorious headway by force of arms. Ideas must be combatted by ideas, and it is only by the propaganda of the idea that we can prepare humanity for its future. Violence is always a means of preventing the sincere and fruitful diffusion of an idea. We do not say this merely for the abnormals of the lower classes. We refer with scientific serenity also to the upper classes, who would suppress by violence every manifestation of revolt against the social iniquities, every affirmation of faith in a better future.

This is the conception of our science, which thus succeeds in distinguishing traits of character even among the unlucky and forlorn people of the criminal world, while the classic school of criminology regards a criminal as a sort of abstract and normal man, with the exception of cases of minors, deaf mutes, inebriates, and maniacs.

In fact, the classic school of criminology regards all thieves as THE thief, all murderers as THE murderer, and the human shape disappears in the mind of the legislator, while it re-appears before the judge. Before the essayist and legislator, the criminal is a sort of moving dummy, on whose hack the judge may paste an article of the penal code. If you leave out of consideration the established cases of exceptional and rare human psychology mentioned in the penal code, all other cases serve the judge merely as an excuse to select from the criminal code the number of that article which will fit the criminal dummy, and if he should paste 404 instead of 407 on its back, the court of appeals would resist, any change of numbers. And if this dummy came to life and said: "The question of my number may be very important for you, but if you would study all the conditions that compelled me to take other people's things, you would realize that this importance is very diagrammatic," the judge would answer: "That's all right for the justice of the future, but it isn't now. You are number 404 of the criminal code, and after leaving this court room with this number pasted legally on your back, you will receive another number, for you will enter prison as number 404 and will exchange it for entry number 1525, or some other, because your personality as a man disappears entirely before the enactment of social justice!" And then it is pretended that this man, whose personality is thus absurdly ignored, should leave prison cured of all degeneration, and if he falls back into the path of thorns of his misery and commits another crime, the judge simply pastes another article over the other, by adding number 80 or 81, which refer to cases of relapse, to number 404!

In this way the classic school of criminology came to its unit of punishment, which it heralded as its great progress. In the Middle Ages, the diversity of punishment was greater. But in the 19th century the classic school of criminology combatted dishonoring punishment, corporeal punishment, confiscation, professional punishment, capital punishment, with its ideal of one sole penalty, the only panacea for crime and criminals, *prison*.

We have, indeed, prohibitory measures and fines even today. But in substance the whole punitive armory is reduced to imprisonment, since fines are likewise convertible into so many days or months of imprisonment. Solitary confinement is the ideal of the classic school of criminology. But experience proves that this penalty has as much effect on the disease of criminality, as the remedy of a physician would have, who would sit in the door of a hospital and tell every patient seeking relief: "Whatever may be your disease, I have only one medicine and that is a decoction of rhubarb. You have heart trouble? Well, then, the problem for me is simply--how big a dose of rhubarb decoction shall I give you?"

And measuring doses of penalty is the foundation of the criminal code. That is so true that this code is in its last analysis but a table of criminal logarithms for figuring out penalties. Woe to the judge who makes a mistake in sentencing a 19 year old offender who was drunk when he sinned, but had premeditated his deed. Woe to the judge, if he misses his calculation in adding or subtracting the third, or sixth, or one half, corresponding to the prescribed extenuating or aggravating circumstances! If he makes a miscalculation, the court of appeals is invoked by the defendant, and the inexorable court of appeals tells the judge: "Figure this over again. You have been unjust." The only question for the judge is this: Add your sums and subtract your deductions, and the prisoner is sentenced to one year, seven months, and thirteen days. Not one day more or less! But the human spectator asks: "If the criminal should happen to be reformed before the expiration of his term, should he be retained in prison?" The judge replies: "I don't care, he stays in one year, seven months, and thirteen days!"

Then the human spectator says: "But suppose the criminal should not yet be fit for human society at the expiration of his term?" The judge replies: "At the expiration of his term he leaves prison, for when he has absolved his last day, he has paid his debt!"

This is the same case as that of the imaginary physician who says: "You have heart trouble? Then take a quart of rhubarb decoction and stay twelve days in the hospital." Another patient says: "I have broken my leg." And the doctor: "All right, take a pint of rhubarb decoction and 17 days in the hospital." A third has inflammation of the lungs, and the doctor prescribes three quarts of rhubarb decoction and three months in the hospital. "But if my inflammation is cured before that time?" "No matter," says the doctor, "you stay in three months." "But if I am not cured of my lung trouble after three months?" "No matter," says the doctor, "you leave after three months."

To such results have wise men been led by a system of penal justice, which is a denial of all elementary common sense. They have forgotten the personality of the criminal and occupied themselves exclusively with crime as an abstract juristic phenomenon. In the same manner, the old style medicine occupied itself with disease as such, as an abstract pathological phenomenon, without taking into account the personality of the patient. The ancient physicians did not consider whether a patient was well or ill nourished, young or old, strong or weak, nervous or full-blooded. They cured fever as fever, pleurisy as pleurisy. Modern medicine, on the other hand, declares that disease must be studied in the living person of the patient. And the same disease may require different treatment, if the condition of the patient is different.

Criminal justice has taken the same historical course of development as medicine. The classic school of criminology is still in the same stage, in which medicine was before the middle of the 19th century. It deals with theft, murder, fraud, as such. But that which claims so much of the attention of society has been forgotten by the classic school. For that school has forgotten to study the murderer, the thief, the forger, and without that study their crimes cannot be understood.

Crime is one of the conditions required for the study of the criminal. But, the same crime may require the application of different remedies to the personalities of different criminals, according to the different anthropological and social conditions of the various criminals. There is a fundamental distinction between the anthropological and social types of criminals, whom I have divided into five categories, which are today unanimously accepted by criminalist anthropologists, since the Geneva congress offered an opportunity to explain the misapprehension which led some foreign scientists to believe that the Italian school regarded one of these types (the born criminal) merely as an organic anomaly.

Just a word concerning each one of these five types.

The **born criminal** is a victim of that which I will call (seeing that science has not yet solved this problem) criminal neurosis, which is very analogous to epileptic neurosis, but which is not in itself sufficient to make one a criminal. Our adversaries had the idea that the mere possession of a crooked nose or a slanting skull stamped a man as predisposed by birth to murder or theft. But a man may he a born criminal, that is to say, he may have some congenital degeneration which predisposes him toward crime, and yet he may die at the age of 80 without having committed any crime, because he was fortunate enough to live in an environment which did not offer him any temptation to commit crime. Again, are not many predisposed toward insanity without ever becoming insane? If the same individual were to live under unfavorable conditions, without any education, if he were to find himself in unhealthy telluric surroundings, in a mine, a rice field, or a miasmatic swamp, he would become insane. But if instead of living in conditions that condemn him to lunacy he were to be under no necessity to struggle for his daily bread, if he could live in affluence, he might exhibit some eccentricity of character, but would not cross the threshold of an insane asylum. The same happens in the case of criminality. One may have a congenital predisposition toward crime, but if he lives in favorable surroundings, he will live to the end of his natural life without violating any criminal or moral law. At any rate we must drop the prejudice that only those are criminals on whose backs the judge has pasted a number. For there are many scoundrels at large who commit crime with impunity, or who brush the edge of the criminal law in the most repulsive immorality without violating it.

This misunderstanding was explained at the congress of Geneva by the statement that the interaction of the social and telluric environment is required also in the case of the born criminal. And now we may take it for granted that my classification of five types is everywhere accepted. These are the following: The **born** *criminal* who has a congenital predisposition for crime; the ***insane criminal*** suffering from some clinical form of mental alienation, and whom even our existing penal code had to recognize; the ***habitual criminal***, that is to say one who has acquired the habit of crime mainly through the ineffective measures employed by society for the prevention and repression of crime. A common figure in our large industrial centers is that of the abandoned child which has to go begging from its earliest youth in order to collect an income for the enterprising boss or for its poor family, without an opportunity to educate its moral sense in the filth of the streets. It is punished for the first time by the law and sent to prison or to a reformatory, where it is inevitably corrupted. Then, when such an individual comes out of prison, he is stigmatized as a thief or forger, watched by the police, and if he secures work in some shop, the owner is indirectly induced to discharge him, so that he must inevitably fall back upon crime.

Thus one acquires crime as a habit, a product of social rottenness, due to the ineffective measures for the prevention and repression of crime. There is furthermore the ***occasional criminal***, who commits very insignificant criminal acts, more because he is led astray by his conditions of life than because the aggressive energy of a degenerate personality impels him. If he is not made worse by a prison life, he may find an opportunity to return to a normal life in society. Finally there is the ***passionate criminal***, who, like the insane criminal, has received attention from the positive school of criminology; which, however, did not come to any definite conclusions regarding him, such as may be gathered by means of the experimental method through study in prisons, insane asylums, or in freedom. The relations between passion and crime have so far been studied on a field in which no solution was possible. For the classic school considers such a crime according to the greater or smaller intensity and violence of passion and comes to the conclusion that the degree of responsibility decreases to the extent that the intensity of a passion increases, and vice versa. The problem cannot be solved in this way. There are passions which may rise to the highest degree of intensity without reducing the responsibility. For instance, is one who murders from motives of revenge a passionate criminal who must be excused?

The classic school of criminology says "No," and for my part I agree with them. Francesco Carrara says: "There are blind passions, and others which are reasonable.

Blind passions deprive one of free will, reasonable ones do not. Blind and excusable passions are fear, honor, love, reasonable and inexcusable ones are hatred and revenge." But how so? I have studied murderers who killed for revenge and who told me that the desire for revenge took hold of them like a fever, so that they "forgot even to eat." Hate and revenge can take possession of a man to such an extent that he becomes blind with passion. The truth is that passion must be considered not so far as its violence or quantity are concerned, but rather as to its quality. We must distinguish between social and anti-social passion, the one favoring the conditions of life for the species and collectivity, the other antagonistic to the development of the collectivity. In the first case, we have love, injured honor, etc, which are passions normally useful to society, and aberrations of which may be excused more or less according to individual cases. On the other hand, we have inexcusable passions, because their psychological tendency is to antagonize the development of society. They are antisocial, and cannot be excused, and hate and revenge are among them.

The positive school therefore admits that a passion is excusable, when the moral sense of a man is normal, when his past record is clear, and when his crime is due to a social passion, which makes it excusable.

We shall see tomorrow what remedies the positive school of criminology proposes for each one of these categories of criminals, in distinction from the measuring of doses of imprisonment advocated by the classic school.

We have thus exhausted in a short and general review the subject of the natural origin of criminality.--To sum up, crime is a social phenomenon, due to the interaction of anthropological, telluric, and social factors. This law brings about what I have called criminal saturation, which means that every society has the criminality which it deserves, and which produces by means of its geographical and social conditions such quantities and qualities of crime as correspond to the development of each collective human group.

Thus the old saying of Imetelet is confirmed: "There is an annual balance of crime, which must be paid and settled with greater regularity than the accounts of the national revenue." However, we positivists give to this statement a less fatalistic interpretation, since we have demonstrated that crime is not our immutable destiny, even though it is a vain beginning to attempt to attenuate or eliminate crime by mere schemes. The truth is that the balance of crime is determined by the physical and social environment. But by changing the condition of the social environment, which is most easily modified, the legislator may alter the influence of the telluric environment and the organic and psychic conditions of the population, control the greater portion of crimes, and reduce them considerably. It is our firm conviction that a truly civilized legislator can attenuate the plague of criminality, not so much by means of the criminal code, as by means of remedies which are latent in the remainder of the social life and of legislation. And the experience of the most advanced countries confirms this by the beneficent and preventive influence of criminal legislation resting on efficacious social reforms.

We arrive, then, at this scientific conclusion: In the society of the future, the necessity for penal justice will be reduced to the extent that social justice grows intensively and extensively.

III.

In the preceding two lectures, I have given you a short review of the new current in scientific thought, which studies the painful and dangerous phenomena of criminality. We must now draw the logical conclusions, in theory and practice, from the teachings of experimented science, for the removal of the gangrenous plague of crime. Under the influence of the positive methods of research, the old formula "Science for science's sake" has given place to the new formula "Science for life's sake." For it would be useless for the human mind to retreat into the vault of philosophical concentration, if this intellectual mastery did not produce as a counter-effect a beneficent wave of real improvement in the destinies of the human race.

What, then, has the civilized world to offer in the way of remedies against criminality? The classic school of criminology, being unable to locate in the course of its scientific and historical mission the natural causes of crime, as I have shown in the preceding lectures, was not in a position to deal in a comprehensive and far-seeing manner with this problem of the remedy against criminality. Some of the classic criminologists, such as Bentham, Romagnosi, or Ellero, with a more positive bent of mind than others, may have given a little of their scientific activity to the analysis of this problem, namely the prevention of crime. But Ellero himself had to admit that "the classic school of criminology has written volumes concerning the death penalty and torture, but has produced but a few pages on the prevention of criminality." The historical mission of that school consisted in a reduction of punishment. For being born on the eve of the French revolution in the name of individualism and natural rights, it was a protest against the barbarian penalties of the Middle Ages. And thus the practical and glorious result of the classic school was a propaganda for the abolition of the most brutal penalties of the Middle Ages, such as the death penalty, torture, mutilation. We in our turn now follow up the practical and scientific mission of the classic school of criminology with a still more noble and fruitful mission by adding to the problem of the ***diminution of penalties*** the problem of the ***diminution of crimes***. It is worth more to humanity to reduce the number of crimes than to reduce the dread sufferings of criminal punishments, although even this is a noble work, after the evil plant of crime has been permitted to grow in the realm of life. Take, for instance, the philanthropic awakening due to the Congress of Geneva in the matter of the Red Cross Society, for the care, treatment and cure of the wounded in war. However noble and praiseworthy this mission may be, it would be far nobler and better to prevent war than to heal the mutilated and wounded. If the same zeal and persistence, which have been expended in the work of the Red Cross Society, had been devoted to the realization of international brotherhood, the weary road of human progress would show far better results.

It is a noble mission to oppose the ferocious penalties of the Middle Ages. But it is still nobler to forestall crime. The classic school of criminology directed its attention merely to penalties, to repressive measures after crime had been committed, with all its terrible moral and material consequences. For in the classic school, the remedies against criminality have not the social aim of improving human life, but merely the illusory mission of retributive justice, meeting a moral delinquency by a corresponding punishment in the shape of legal sentences. This is the spirit which is still pervading criminal legislation, although there is a sort of eclectic compromise between the old and the new. The classic school of criminology has substituted for the old absolutist conceptions of justice the eclectic theory that absolute justice has the right to punish, but a right modified by the interests of civilized life in present society. This is the point discussed in Italy in the celebrated controversy between Pasquale Stanislao Mancini and Terencio Mamiani, in 1847. This is in substance the theory followed by the classic criminologists who revised the penal code, which public opinion considers incapable of protecting society against the dangers of crime. And we have but to look about us in the realities of contemporaneous life in order to see that the criminal code is far from being a remedy against crime, that it remedies nothing, because either premeditation or passion in the person of the criminal deprive the criminal law of all prohibitory power. The deceptive faith in the efficacy of criminal law still lives in the public mind, because every normal man feels that the thought of imprisonment would stand in his way, if he contemplated tomorrow committing a theft, a rape, or a murder. He feels the bridle of the social sense. And the criminal code lends more strength to it and holds him back from criminal actions. But even if the criminal code did not exist, he would not commit a crime, so long as his physical and social environment would not urge him in that direction. The criminal code serves only to isolate temporarily from social intercourse those who are not considered worthy of it. And this punishment prevents the criminal for a while from repeating his criminal deed. But it is evident that the punishment is not imposed until after the deed has been done. It is a remedy directed against effects, but it does not touch the causes, the roots, of the evil.

We may say that in social life penalties have the same relation to crime that medicine has to disease. After a disease has developed in an organism, we have recourse to a physician. But he cannot do anything else but to reach the effects in some single individual. On the other hand, if the individual and the collectivity had obeyed the rules of preventive hygiene, the disease would have been avoided 90 times in 100, and would have appeared only in extreme and exceptional cases, where a wound or an organic condition break through the laws of health. Lack of providence on the part of man, which is due to insufficient expression of the forces of the intellect and pervades so large a part of human life, is certainly to blame for the fact that mankind chooses to use belated remedies rather than to observe the laws of health, which demand a greater methodical control of one's actions and more foresight, because the remedy must be applied before the disease becomes apparent. I say occasionally that human society acts in the matter of criminality with the same lack of forethought that most people do in the matter of tooth-ache. How many individuals do not suffer from tooth-ache, especially in the great cities? And yet any one convinced of the miraculous power of hygiene could easily clean his teeth every day and prevent the microbes of tooth rot from thriving, thereby saving his teeth from harm and pain. But it is tedious to do this every day. It implies a control of one's self. It cannot be done without the scientific conviction that induces men to acquire this habit. Most people say: "Oh well, if that tooth rots, I'll bear the pain." But when the night comes in which they cannot sleep for toothache, they will swear at themselves for not having taken precautions and will run to the dentist, who in most cases cannot help them any more.

The legislator should apply the rules of social hygiene in order to reach the roots of criminality. But this would require that he should bring his mind and will to bear daily on a legislative reform of individual and social life, in the field of economics and morals as well as in that of administration, politics, and intelligence. Instead of that, the legislators permit the microbes of criminality to develop their pathogenic powers in society. When crimes become manifest, the legislator knows no other remedy but imprisonment in order to punish an evil which he should have prevented. Unfortunately this scientific conviction is not yet rooted and potent in the minds of the legislators of most of the civilized countries, because they represent on an average the backward scientific convictions of one or two previous generations. The legislator who sits in parliament today was the university student of 30 years ago. With a few very rare exceptions he is supplied only with knowledge of outgrown scientific research. It is a historical law that the work of the legislator is always behind the science of his time. But nevertheless the scientist has the urgent duty to spread the conviction that hygiene is worth as much on the field of civilization as it is in medicine for the public health.

This is the fundamental conviction at which the positive school arrives: That which has happened in medicine will happen in criminology. The great value of practical hygiene, especially of social hygiene, which is greater than that of individual hygiene, has been recognized after the marvelous scientific discoveries concerning the origin and primitive causes of the most dangerous diseases. So long as Pasteur and his disciples had not given to the world their discovery of the pathogenic microbes of all infectious diseases, such as typhoid fever, cholera, diphtheria, tuberculosis, etc, more or less absurd remedies were demanded of the science of medicine. I remember, for instance, that I was compelled in my youth, during an epidemic of cholera, to stay in a closed room, in which fumigation was carried on with substances irritating the bronchial tubes and lungs without killing the cholera microbes, as was proved later on. It was not until the real causes of those infectious diseases were discovered, that efficient remedies could be employed against them. An aqueduct given to a center of population like Naples is a better protection against cholera than drugs, even after the disease has taken root in the midst of the people of Naples. This is the modern lesson which we wish to teach in the field of criminology, a field which will always retain its repressive functions as an exceptional and ultimate refuge, because we do not believe that we shall succeed in eliminating all forms of criminality. Hence, if a crime manifests itself, repression may be employed as one of the remedies of criminology, but it should be the very last, not the exclusively dominating one, as it is today.

It is this blind worship of punishment which is to blame for the spectacle which we witness in every modern country, the spectacle that the legislators neglect the rules of social hygiene and wake up with a start when some form of crime becomes acute, and that they know of no better remedy than an intensification of punishment meeted out by the penal code. If one year of imprisonment is not enough, we'll make it ten years, and if an aggravation of the ordinary penalty is not enough, we'll pass a law of exception. It is always the blind trust in punishment which remains the only remedy of the public conscience and which always works to the detriment of morality and material welfare, because it does not save the society of honest people and strikes without curing those who have fallen a prey to guilt and crime.

The positive school of criminology, then, aside from the greater value attributed to daily and systematic measures of social hygiene for the prevention of criminality, comes to radically different conclusions also in the matter of repressive justice. The classic school has for a cardinal remedy against crime a preference for one kind of punishment, namely imprisonment, and gives fixed and prescribed doses of this remedy. It is the logical conclusion of retributive justice that it travels by way of an illusory purification from moral guilt to the legal responsibility of the criminal and thence on to a corresponding dose of punishment, which has been previously prescribed and fixed.

We, on the other hand, hold that even the surviving form of repression, which will be inevitable in spite of the application of the rules of social prevention, should be widely different, on account of the different conception which we have of crime and of penal justice.

In the majority of cases composed of minor crimes committed by people belonging to the most numerous and least dangerous class of occasional or passionate criminals, the only form of civil repression will be ***the compensation of the victim for his loss***. According to us, this should he the only form of penalty imposed in the majority of minor crimes committed by people who are not dangerous. In the present practice of justice the compensation of the victim for his loss has become a laughing stock, because this victim is systematically forgotten. The whole attention of the classic school has been concentrated on the juridical entity of the crime. The victim of the crime has been forgotten, although this victim deserves philanthropic sympathy more than the criminal who has done the harm. It is true, every, judge adds to the sentence the formula that the criminal is responsible for the injury and the costs to another authority. But the process of law puts off this compensation to an indefinite time, and if the victim succeeds a few years after the passing of the sentence in getting any action on the matter, the criminal has in the meantime had a thousand legal subterfuges to get away with his spoils. And thus the law itself becomes the breeding ground of personal revenge, for Filangieri says aptly that an innocent man grasps the dagger of the murderer, when the sword of justice does not defend him.

Let us say at this point that the rigid application of compensation for damages should never be displaced by imprisonment, because this would be equivalent to sanctioning a real class distinction, for the rich can laugh at damages, while the proletarian would have to make good a sentence of 1000 lire by 100 days in prison, and in the meantime the innocent family that tearfully waits for him outside, would be plunged into desperate straits. Compensation for damages should never take place in any other way than by means of the labor of the prisoner to an extent satisfactory to the family of the injured. It has been attempted to place this in an eclectic way on our law books, but this proposition remains a dead letter and is not applied in Italy, because a stroke of legislator's pen is not enough to change the fate of an entire nation.

These practical and efficient measures would be taken in the case of lesser criminals. For the graver crimes committed by atavistic or congenital criminals, of by persons inclining toward crime from acquired habit or mental alienation, the positive school of criminology reserves segregation for an indefinite time, for it is absurd to fix the time beforehand in the case of a dangerous degenerate who has committed a grave crime.

The question of indeterminate sentences has been recently discussed also by Pessina, who combats it, of course, because the essence of the classic school of criminology is retribution for a fault by means of corresponding punishment. We might reply that no human judge can use any other but the grossest scale by which to determine whether you are responsible to the extent of the whole, one half, or one third. And since there is no absolute or objective criterion by which the ratio of crime to punishment can be determined, penal justice becomes a game of chance. But we content ourselves by pointing out that segregation for an indefinite time has so much truth in it, that even the most orthodox of the classic school admit it, for instance in the case of criminals under age. Now, if an indeterminate sentence is a violation of the principles of the classic school, I cannot understand why it can be admitted in the case of minors, but not in the case of adults. This is evidently an expedient imposed by the exigencies of practical life, and only the positive school of criminology can meet them by a logical systematization. For the rest, indefinite segregation, such as we propose for the most dangerous atavistic criminals, is a measure which is already in use for ordinary lunatics as well us for criminal lunatics. But it may be said that this is an administrative measure, not a court sentence. Well, if any one is so fond of formulas as to make this objection, he may get all the fun out of them that he likes. But it is a fact that an insane person who has committed a crime is sent to a building with iron bars on its gates such as a prison has. You may call it an administrative building or a penal institute, the name is unessential, for the substance alone counts. We maintain that congenital or pathological criminals cannot be locked up for a definite term in any institution, but should remain there until they are adapted for the normal life of society.

This radical reform of principles carries with it a radical transformation of details. Given an indeterminate segregation, there should be organs of guardianship for persons so secluded, for instance permanent committees for the periodical revision of sentences. In the future, the criminal judge will always secure ample evidence to prove whether a defendant is really guilty, for this is the fundamental point. If it is certain that he has committed the crime, he should either be excluded from social intercourse or sentenced to mate good the damage, provided the criminal is not dangerous and the crime not grave. It is absurd to sentence a man to five or six days imprisonment for some insignificant misdemeanor. You lower him in the eyes of the public, subject him to surveillance by the police, and send him to prison from whence he will go out more corrupted than he was on entering it. It is absurd to impose segregation in prison for small errors. Compensation for injuries is enough.

For the segregation of the graver criminals, the management must be as scientific as it is now in insane asylums. It is absurd to place an old pensioned soldier or a hardened bureaucrat at the head of a penal institution. It is enough to visit one of those compulsory human beehives and to see how a military discipline carries a brutal hypocrisy into it. The management of such institutions must be scientific, and the care of their inmates must be scientific, since a grave crime is always a manifestation of the pathological condition of the individual. In America there are already institutions, such as the Elmira Reformatory, where the application of the methods of the positive school of criminology has been solemnly promised. The director of the institution is a psychologist, a physician. When a criminal under age is brought in, he is studied from the point of view of physiology and psychology. The treatment serves to regenerate the plants who, being young, may still be straightened up. Scientific therapeutics can do little for relapsed criminals. The present repression of crime robs the prisoner of his personality and reduces him to a number, either in mass imprisonment which corrupts him completely, or in solitary confinement, which will turn him into a stupid or raving beast.

These methods are also gradually introduced in the insane asylums. I must tell you a little story to illustrate this. When I was a professor in Pisa, eight years ago, I took my students to the penitentiaries and the asylum for the criminal insane in Montelupo, as I always used to do. Dr. Algieri, the director of this asylum, showed us among others a very interesting case. This was a man of about 45, whose history was shortly the following: He was a bricklayer living in one of the cities of Toscana. He had been a normal and honest man, a very good father, until one unlucky day came, in which a brick falling from a factory broke a part of his skull. He fell down unconscious, was picked up, carried to the hospital, and cured of his external injury, but lost both his physical and moral health. He became an epileptic.

And the lesion to which the loss of the normal function of his nervous system was due transformed him from the docile and even-tempered man that he had been into a quarrelsome and irritable individual, so that he was less regular in his work, less moral and honest in his family life, and was finally sentenced for a grave assault in a saloon brawl. He was condemned as a common criminal to I don't know how many years of imprisonment. But in prison, the exceptional conditions of seclusion brought on a deterioration of his physical and moral health, his epileptic fits became more frequent, his character grew worse. The director of the prison sent him to the asylum for the insane criminals at Montelupo, which shelters criminals suspected of insanity and insane criminals.

Dr. Algieri studied the interesting case and came to the diagnosis that there was splinter of bone in the man's brain which had not been noticed in the treatment at the hospital, and that this was the cause of the epilepsy and demoralization of the prisoner. He trepanned a portion of the skull around the old wound and actually found a bone splinter lodged in the man's brain. He removed the splinter, and put a platinum plate over the trepanned place to protect the brain. The man improved, the epileptic fits ceased, his moral condition became as normal as before, and this bricklayer (how about the free will?) was dismissed from the asylum, for he had given proofs of normal behavior for about five or six months, thanks to the wisdom of the doctor who had relieved him of the lesion which had made him epileptic and immoral. If this asylum for insane criminals had not been in existence, he would have ended in a padded cell, the same as another man whom I and my students saw a few years ago in the Ancona penitentiary. The director, an old soldier, said to me: "Professor, I shall show you a type of human beast. He is a man who passes four fifths of the year in a padded cell." After calling six attendants, "because we must be careful," we went to the cell, and I said to that director: "Please, leave this man to me. I have little faith in the existence of human beasts. Keep the attendants at a distance." "No," replied the director, "my responsibility does not permit me to do that."

But I insisted. The cell was opened, and the man came out of it really like a wild beast with bulging eyes and distorted face. But I met him with a smile and said to him kindly: "How are you?" This change of treatment immediately changed the attitude of the man. He first had a nervous fit and then broke into tears and told me his story with the eloquence of suffering. He said that he had some days in which he was not master of himself, but he recognized that he was good whenever the attacks of temper were over. Without saying so, he thus invoked the wisdom of human psychology for better treatment. There is indeed a physician in those prisons, but he treats generally only the ordinary diseases and is not familiar with special psychological knowledge. There may be exceptions, and in that case it is a lucky coincidence. But the prison doctor has also his practice outside and hurries through his prison work. "They simulate sickness in order to get out of prison," he says. And this will be so all the more that the physicians of our time have not sufficient training in psychology to enable them to do justice to the psychology of the criminal.

You must, therefore, give a scientific management to these institutions, and you will then render humane even the treatment of those grave and dangerous criminals, whose condition cannot be met by a simple compensation of the injury they have done to others.

This is the function of repression as we look upon it, an inevitable result of the positive data regarding the natural origin of crime.

We believe, in other words, that repression will play but an unimportant role in the future. We believe that every branch of legislation will come to prefer the remedies of social hygiene to those symptomatic remedies and apply them from day to day. And thus we come to the theory of the prevention of crime. Some say: "it is better to repress than to prevent." Others say: "It is better to prevent than to repress." In order to solve this conflict we must remember that there are two widely different kinds of repression. There is the immediate, direct empirical repression, which does not investigate the cause of criminality, but waits until the crime is about to be committed. That is police prevention. There is on the other hand a social prevention which has an indirect and more remote function, which does not wait until crime is about to be committed, but locates the causes of crime in poverty, abandoned children, trampdom, etc, and seeks to prevent these conditions by remote and indirect means. In Italy, prevention is anonymous with arrest. That is to say, by repression is understood only police repression. Under these circumstances, it is well to take it for granted that some of the expected crimes will be carried out, for crimes are not committed at fixed periods after first informing the police. The damage done by criminality, and especially by political and social criminality, against which police repression is particularly directed, will be smaller than that done by the abuse inseparably connected with police power. In the case of atavistic criminality, prevention does not mean handcuffing of the man who is about to commit a crime, but devising such economic and educational measures in the family and administration as will eliminate the causes of crime or attenuate them, precisely because punishment is less effective than prevention.

In other words, in order to prevent crime, we must have recourse to measures which I have called "substitutes for punishment," and which prevent, the development of crime, because they go to the source in order to do away with effects.

Bentham narrates that the postal service in England, in the 18th century, was in the hands of stage drivers, but this service was not connected with the carrying of passengers, as became the custom later. And then it was impossible to get the drivers to arrive on time, because they stopped too often at the inns. Fines were imposed, imprisonment was resorted to, yet the drivers arrived late. The penalties did not accomplish any results so long as the causes remained. Then the idea was conceived to carry passengers on the postal stages, and that stopped the drivers from being late, because whenever they made a halt, the passengers, who had an interest in arriving on time, called the drivers and did not give them much time to linger. This is an illustration of a substitute for punishment.

Another illustration. In the Middle Ages, up to the eve of our modern civilization, piracy was in vogue. Is there anything that was not tried to suppress piracy? The pirates were persecuted like wild beasts. Whenever they were caught they were condemned to the most terrible forms of death. Yet piracy continued. Then came the application of steam navigation, and piracy disappeared as by magic. And robbery and brigandage? They withstood the death penalty and extraordinary raids by soldiers. And we witness today the spectacle of a not very serious contest between the police who wants to catch a brigand, Musolino; and a brigand who does not wish to be caught.

Wherever the woods are not traversed by railroads or tramways, brigandage carries on its criminal trade. But wherever railroads and tramways exist, brigandage is a form of crime which disappears. You may insist on death penalties and imprisonment, but assault and robbery will continue, because it is connected with geographical conditions. Use on the other hand the instrument of civilization, without sentencing any one, and brigandage and robbery will disappear before its light. And if human beings in large industrial centers are herded together in tenements and slum hotels, how can a humane judge aggravate the penalties against sexual crimes? How can the sense of shame develop among people, when young and old of both sexes are crowded together in the same bed, in the same corrupted and corrupting environment, which robs the human soul of every noble spark?

I might stray pretty far, if I were to continue these illustrations of social hygiene which will be the true solution of the problem and the supreme systematic, daily humane, and bloodless remedy against the disease of criminality. However, we have not the simple faith that in the near or far future of humanity crimes can ever be wholly eradicated. Even Socialism, which looks forward to a fundamental transformation of future society on the basis of brotherhood and social justice, cannot elevate itself to the absolute and naive faith that criminality, insanity, and suicide can ever fully disappear from the earth. But it is our firm conviction that the endemic form of criminality, insanity, and suicide will disappear, and that nothing will remain of them but rare sporadic forms caused by lesion or telluric and other influences.

Since we have made the great discovery that malaria, which weighs upon so many parts in Italy, is dependent for its transmission on a certain mosquito, we have acquired the control of malarial therapeutics and are enabled to protect individuals and families effectively against malaria. But aside from this function of protecting people, there must be a social prevention, and since those malarial insects can live only in swampy districts, it is necessary to bring to those unreclaimed lands the blessing of the hoe and plow, in order to remove the cause and do away with the effects. The same problem confronts us in criminology. In the society of the future we shall undertake this work of social hygiene, and thereby we shall remove the epidemic forms of criminality. And nine-tenths of the crimes will then disappear, so that nothing will remain of them but exceptional cases. There will remain, for instance, such cases as that of the bricklayer which I mentioned, because there may always be accidents, no matter what may be the form of social organization, and nervous disorders may thus appear in certain individuals. But you can see that these would be exceptional cases of criminality, which will be easily cured under the direction of science, that will be the supreme and beneficent manager of institutes for the segregation of those who will be unfit for social intercourse. The problem of criminality will thus be solved as far as possible, because the gradual transformation of society will eliminate the swamps in which the miasma of crime may form and breed.

If we wish to apply these standards to an example which today attracts the attention of all Italy to this noble city, if we desire to carry our theories into the practice of contemporaneous life, if science is to respond to the call of life, let us throw a glance at that form of endemic criminality known as the Camorra in this city, which has taken root here just as stabbing affrays have in certain centers of Turin, and the Mafia in certain centers of Sicily. In the first place, we must not be wilfully blind to facts and refuse to see that the citizens will protect themselves, if social justice does not do so. And from that to crime there is but a shot step. But which is the swampy soil in which this social disease can spread and persist like leprosy in tin collective organism? It is the economic poverty of the masses, which lends to intellectual and moral poverty.

You have lately had in Naples a very fortunate struggle, which seems to have overcome one of the representatives of the high Camorra. But can we believe that the courageous work of a few public writers has touched the roots of the Camorra in this city? It would be self-deception to think so. For we see that plants blossom out again, even after the most destructive hurricane has passed over them.

The healing of society is not so easy, that a collective plague may be cured by the courageous acts of one or more individuals. The process is much slower and more complicated. Nevertheless these episodes are milestones of victory in the on-ward march of civilization, which will paralyze the historical manifestations of so-cial criminality. Here, then, we have a city in which some hundred thousand people rise every morning and do not know how to get a living, who have no fixed occupa-tion, because there is not enough industrial development to reach that methodical application of labor which lifted humanity out of the prehistoric forests. Truly, the human race progresses by two uplifting energies: War and labor.

In primitive and savage society, when the human personality did not know the check of social discipline, a military discipline held the members of the tribe together. But war, while useful in primitive society, loses its usefulness more and more, because it carries within itself the cancer that paralyzes it.

While war compels collective groups to submit to the co-ordinating discipline of human activity, it also decreases the respect for human life. The soldier who kills his fellow man of a neighboring nation by a stroke of his sword will easily lose the respect for the life of members of his own social group. Then the second educational energy interferes, the energy of labor, which makes itself felt at the decisive moment of prehistoric development, when the human race passes from a pastoral, hunting, and nomadic life Into an agriculture and settled life. This is the historic stage, in which the collective ownership of land and instruments of production is displaced by communal property, family property, and finally individual property. During these stages, humanity passes from individual and isolated labor in collective, associated, co-ordinated labor. The remains of the neolithic epoch show us the progress of the first workshops, in which our ancestors gathered and fashioned their primitive tools and arms. They give us an idea of associated and common labor, which then becomes the great uplifting energy, because, unlike war, it does not carry within itself a disdain or violation of the rights of others. Labor is the sole perennial energy of mankind which leads to social perfection. But if you have 100,000 persons in a city like Naples who do not enjoy the certainty and discipline of employment at methodical and common labor, you need not wonder that the uncertainty of daily life, an illfed stomach, and an anemic brain, result in the atrophy of all moral sentiment, and that the evil plant of the Camorra spreads out over everything. The processes in the law courts may attract the fleeting attention of public opinion, of legislation, of government, to the disease from which this portion of the social organism is suffering, but mere repression will not accomplish anything lasting.

The teaching of science tells us plainly that in such a case of endemic criminality social remedies must be applied to social evils. Unless the remedy of social reforms accompanies the development and protection of labor; unless justice is assured to every member of the collectivity, the courage of this or that citizen is spent in vain, and the evil plant will continue to thrive in the jungle.

Taught by the masterly and inflexible logic of facts, we come to the adoption of the scientific method in criminal research and conclude that a simple and uniform remedy like punishment is not adequate to cure such a natural and social phenomenon as crime, which has its own natural and social causes. The measures for the preservation of society against criminality must be manifold, complex and varied, and must be the outcome of persevering and systematic work on the part of legislators and citizens on the solid foundation of a systematic collective economy.

Let me take leave of you with this practical conclusion, and give my heart freedom to send to my brain a wave of fervent blood, which shall express my enduring gratitude for the reception which you have given me. Old in years, but young in spirit and energetic aspiration to every high ideal, I tender you my sincere thanks.

As a man and a citizen, I thank you, because these three lectures have been for me a fountain of youth, of faith, of enthusiasm. Thanks to them I return to the other fields of my daily occupation with a greater faith in the future of my country and of humanity. To you, young Italy, I address these words of thanks, glad and honored, if my words have aroused in your soul one breath which will make you stronger and more confident in the future of civilization and social justice.

The Codes Of Hammurabi And Moses
W. W. Davies

QTY

The discovery of the Hammurabi Code is one of the greatest achievements of archaeology, and is of paramount interest, not only to the student of the Bible, but also to all those interested in ancient history...

Religion   **ISBN:** *1-59462-338-4*   **Pages:132**
MSRP $12.95

The Theory of Moral Sentiments
Adam Smith

QTY

This work from 1749. contains original theories of conscience amd moral judgment and it is the foundation for systemof morals.

Philosophy **ISBN:** *1-59462-777-0*   **Pages:536**
MSRP $19.95

Jessica's First Prayer
Hesba Stretton

QTY

In a screened and secluded corner of one of the many railway-bridges which span the streets of London there could be seen a few years ago, from five o'clock every morning until half past eight, a tidily set-out coffee-stall, consisting of a trestle and board, upon which stood two large tin cans, with a small fire of charcoal burning under each so as to keep the coffee boiling during the early hours of the morning when the work-people were thronging into the city on their way to their daily toil...

Childrens   **ISBN:** *1-59462-373-2*   **Pages:84**
MSRP $9.95

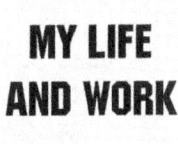

My Life and Work
Henry Ford

QTY

Henry Ford revolutionized the world with his implementation of mass production for the Model T automobile. Gain valuable business insight into his life and work with his own auto-biography... "We have only started on our development of our country we have not as yet, with all our talk of wonderful progress, done more than scratch the surface. The progress has been wonderful enough but..."

Biographies/   **ISBN:** *1-59462-198-5*   **Pages:300**
MSRP $21.95

The Art of Cross-Examination
Francis Wellman

QTY

I presume it is the experience of every author, after his first book is published upon an important subject, to be almost overwhelmed with a wealth of ideas and illustrations which could readily have been included in his book, and which to his own mind, at least, seem to make a second edition inevitable. Such certainly was the case with me; and when the first edition had reached its sixth impression in five months, I rejoiced to learn that it seemed to my publishers that the book had met with a sufficiently favorable reception to justify a second and considerably enlarged edition. ...

Reference   **ISBN:** *1-59462-647-2*

Pages:412

MSRP $19.95

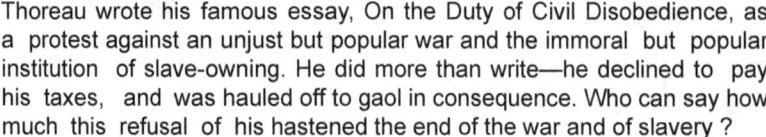

On the Duty of Civil Disobedience
Henry David Thoreau

QTY

Thoreau wrote his famous essay, On the Duty of Civil Disobedience, as a protest against an unjust but popular war and the immoral but popular institution of slave-owning. He did more than write—he declined to pay his taxes, and was hauled off to gaol in consequence. Who can say how much this refusal of his hastened the end of the war and of slavery ?

Law   **ISBN:** *1-59462-747-9*

Pages:48

MSRP $7.45

Dream Psychology Psychoanalysis for Beginners
Sigmund Freud

QTY

Sigmund Freud, born Sigismund Schlomo Freud (May 6, 1856 - September 23, 1939), was a Jewish-Austrian neurologist and psychiatrist who co-founded the psychoanalytic school of psychology. Freud is best known for his theories of the unconscious mind, especially involving the mechanism of repression; his redefinition of sexual desire as mobile and directed towards a wide variety of objects; and his therapeutic techniques, especially his understanding of transference in the therapeutic relationship and the presumed value of dreams as sources of insight into unconscious desires.

Psychology   **ISBN:** *1-59462-905-6*

Pages:196

MSRP $15.45

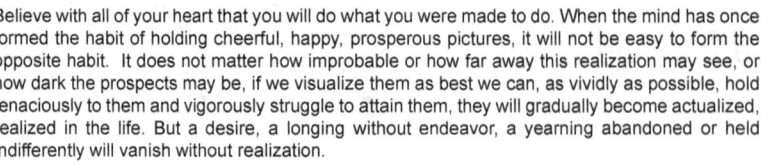

The Miracle of Right Thought
Orison Swett Marden

QTY

Believe with all of your heart that you will do what you were made to do. When the mind has once formed the habit of holding cheerful, happy, prosperous pictures, it will not be easy to form the opposite habit. It does not matter how improbable or how far away this realization may see, or how dark the prospects may be, if we visualize them as best we can, as vividly as possible, hold tenaciously to them and vigorously struggle to attain them, they will gradually become actualized, realized in the life. But a desire, a longing without endeavor, a yearning abandoned or held indifferently will vanish without realization.

Self Help   **ISBN:** *1-59462-644-8*

Pages:360

MSRP $25.45

QTY

The Rosicrucian Cosmo-Conception Mystic Christianity by *Max Heindel*　　ISBN: *1-59462-188-8*　**$38.95**
The Rosicrucian Cosmo-conception is not dogmatic, neither does it appeal to any other authority than the reason of the student. It is: not controversial,
but is: sent forth in the, hope that it may help to clear...　　　　　　　　　　　　　　　　　　　New Age/Religion Pages 646

Abandonment To Divine Providence by *Jean-Pierre de Caussade*　　ISBN: *1-59462-228-0*　**$25.95**
"The Rev. Jean Pierre de Caussade was one of the most remarkable spiritual writers of the Society of Jesus in France in the 18th Century. His death took
place at Toulouse in 1751. His works have gone through many editions and have been republished...　　　　Inspirational/Religion Pages 400

Mental Chemistry by *Charles Haanel*　　　　　　　　　　　　　　　　ISBN: *1-59462-192-6*　**$23.95**
Mental Chemistry allows the change of material conditions by combining and appropriately utilizing the power of the mind. Much like applied chemistry
creates something new and unique out of careful combinations of chemicals the mastery of mental chemistry...　　　　New Age Pages 354

The Letters of Robert Browning and Elizabeth Barret Barrett 1845-1846 vol II　　ISBN: *1-59462-193-4*　**$35.95**
by *Robert Browning* and *Elizabeth Barrett*　　　　　　　　　　　　　　　　　　　Biographies Pages 596

Gleanings In Genesis (volume I) by *Arthur W. Pink*　　　　　　　ISBN: *1-59462-130-6*　**$27.45**
Appropriately has Genesis been termed "the seed plot of the Bible" for in it we have, in germ form, almost all of the great doctrines which are afterwards
fully developed in the books of Scripture which follow...　　　　　　　　　　　　　　Religion/Inspirational Pages 420

The Master Key by *L. W. de Laurence*　　　　　　　　　　　　　　ISBN: *1-59462-001-6*　**$30.95**
In no branch of human knowledge has there been a more lively increase of the spirit of research during the past few years than in the study of Psychology,
Concentration and Mental Discipline. The requests for authentic lessons in Thought Control, Mental Discipline and...　　New Age/Business Pages 422

The Lesser Key Of Solomon Goetia by *L. W. de Laurence*　　　ISBN: *1-59462-092-X*　**$9.95**
This translation of the first book of the "Lernegton" which is now for the first time made accessible to students of Talismanic Magic was done, after careful
collation and edition, from numerous Ancient Manuscripts in Hebrew, Latin, and French...　　　　　New Age/Occult Pages 92

Rubaiyat Of Omar Khayyam by *Edward Fitzgerald*　　　　　　　ISBN:*1-59462-332-5*　**$13.95**
Edward Fitzgerald, whom the world has already learned, in spite of his own efforts to remain within the shadow of anonymity, to look upon as one of the
rarest poets of the century, was born at Bredfield, in Suffolk, on the 31st of March, 1809. He was the third son of John Purcell...　　Music Pages 172

Ancient Law by *Henry Maine*　　　　　　　　　　　　　　　　　　ISBN: *1-59462-128-4*　**$29.95**
The chief object of the following pages is to indicate some of the earliest ideas of mankind, as they are reflected in Ancient Law, and to point out the
relation of those ideas to modern thought.　　　　　　　　　　　　　　　　　　Religion/History Pages 452

Far-Away Stories by *William J. Locke*　　　　　　　　　　　　　　ISBN: *1-59462-129-2*　**$19.45**
"Good wine needs no bush, but a collection of mixed vintages does. And this book is just such a collection. Some of the stories I do not want to remain
buried for ever in the museum files of dead magazine-numbers an author's not unpardonable vanity..."　　　　Fiction Pages 272

Life of David Crockett by *David Crockett*　　　　　　　　　　　　ISBN: *1-59462-250-7*　**$27.45**
"Colonel David Crockett was one of the most remarkable men of the times in which he lived. Born in humble life, but gifted with a strong will, an
indomitable courage, and unremitting perseverance...　　　　　　　　　　　　　Biographies/New Age Pages 424

Lip-Reading by *Edward Nitchie*　　　　　　　　　　　　　　　　　ISBN: *1-59462-206-X*　**$25.95**
Edward B. Nitchie, founder of the New York School for the Hard of Hearing, now the Nitchie School of Lip-Reading, Inc, wrote "LIP-READING Principles
and Practice". The development and perfecting of this meritorious work on lip-reading was an undertaking...　　　　How-to Pages 400

A Handbook of Suggestive Therapeutics, Applied Hypnotism, Psychic Science　　ISBN: *1-59462-214-0*　**$24.95**
by *Henry Munro*　　　　　　　　　　　　　　　　　　　Health/New Age/Health/Self-help Pages 376

A Doll's House: and Two Other Plays by *Henrik Ibsen*　　　　　ISBN: *1-59462-112-8*　**$19.95**
Henrik Ibsen created this classic when in revolutionary 1848 Rome. Introducing some striking concepts in playwriting for the realist genre, this play
has been studied the world over.　　　　　　　　　　　　　　　　　　Fiction/Classics/Plays 308

The Light of Asia by *sir Edwin Arnold*　　　　　　　　　　　　　ISBN: *1-59462-204-3*　**$13.95**
In this poetic masterpiece, Edwin Arnold describes the life and teachings of Buddha. The man who was to become known as Buddha to the world was
born as Prince Gautama of India but he rejected the worldly riches and abandoned the reigns of power when... Religion/History/Biographies Pages 170

The Complete Works of Guy de Maupassant by *Guy de Maupassant*　　ISBN: *1-59462-157-8*　**$16.95**
"For days and days, nights and nights, I had dreamed of that first kiss which was to consecrate our engagement, and I knew not on what spot I should
put my lips..."　　　　　　　　　　　　　　　　　　　Fiction/Classics Pages 240

The Art of Cross-Examination by *Francis L. Wellman*　　　　　ISBN: *1-59462-309-0*　**$26.95**
Written by a renowned trial lawyer, Wellman imparts his experience and uses case studies to explain how to use psychology to extract desired information
through questioning.　　　　　　　　　　　　　　　　　　How-to/Science/Reference Pages 408

Answered or Unanswered? by *Louisa Vaughan*　　　　　　　　ISBN: *1-59462-248-5*　**$10.95**
Miracles of Faith in China　　　　　　　　　　　　　　　　　　　Religion Pages 112

The Edinburgh Lectures on Mental Science (1909) by *Thomas*　　ISBN: *1-59462-008-3*　**$11.95**
This book contains the substance of a course of lectures recently given by the writer in the Queen Street Hail, Edinburgh. Its purpose is to indicate the
Natural Principles governing the relation between Mental Action and Material Conditions...　　　New Age/Psychology Pages 148

Ayesha by *H. Rider Haggard*　　　　　　　　　　　　　　　　　ISBN: *1-59462-301-5*　**$24.95**
Verily and indeed it is the unexpected that happens! Probably if there was one person upon the earth from whom the Editor of this, and of a certain previ-
ous history, did not expect to hear again...　　　　　　　　　　　　　　　　　Classics Pages 380

Ayala's Angel by *Anthony Trollope*　　　　　　　　　　　　　　ISBN: *1-59462-352-X*　**$29.95**
The two girls were both pretty, but Lucy who was twenty-one who supposed to be simple and comparatively unattractive, whereas Ayala was credited, as
her Bombwhat romantic name might show, with poetic charm and a taste for romance. Ayala when her father died was nineteen... Fiction Pages 484

The American Commonwealth by *James Bryce*　　　　　　　　ISBN: *1-59462-286-8*　**$34.45**
An interpretation of American democratic political theory. It examines political mechanics and society from the perspective of Scotsman
James Bryce　　　　　　　　　　　　　　　　　　　Politics Pages 572

Stories of the Pilgrims by *Margaret P. Pumphrey*　　　　　　ISBN: *1-59462-116-0*　**$17.95**
This book explores pilgrims religious oppression in England as well as their escape to Holland and eventual crossing to America on the Mayflower, and
their early days in New England...　　　　　　　　　　　　　　　　　History Pages 268

QTY

The Fasting Cure *by Sinclair Upton*
ISBN: *1-59462-222-1* **$13.95**

In the Cosmopolitan Magazine for May, 1910, and in the Contemporary Review (London) for April, 1910, I published an article dealing with my experiences in fasting. I have written a great many magazine articles, but never one which attracted so much attention... New Age/Self Help/Health Pages 164

Hebrew Astrology *by Sepharial*
ISBN: *1-59462-308-2* **$13.45**

In these days of advanced thinking it is a matter of common observation that we have left many of the old landmarks behind and that we are now pressing forward to greater heights and to a wider horizon than that which represented the mind-content of our progenitors... Astrology Pages 144

Thought Vibration or The Law of Attraction in the Thought World
ISBN: *1-59462-127-6* **$12.95**

by William Walker Atkinson Psychology/Religion Pages 144

Optimism *by Helen Keller*
ISBN: *1-59462-108-X* **$15.95**

Helen Keller was blind, deaf, and mute since 19 months old, yet famously learned how to overcome these handicaps, communicate with the world, and spread her lectures promoting optimism. An inspiring read for everyone... Biographies/Inspirational Pages 84

Sara Crewe *by Frances Burnett*
ISBN: *1-59462-360-0* **$9.45**

In the first place, Miss Minchin lived in London. Her home was a large, dull, tall one, in a large, dull square, where all the houses were alike, and all the sparrows were alike, and where all the door-knockers made the same heavy sound... Childrens/Classic Pages 88

The Autobiography of Benjamin Franklin *by Benjamin Franklin*
ISBN: *1-59462-135-7* **$24.95**

The Autobiography of Benjamin Franklin has probably been more extensively read than any other American historical work, and no other book of its kind has had such ups and downs of fortune. Franklin lived for many years in England, where he was agent... Biographies/History Pages 332

Name	
Email	
Telephone	
Address	
City, State ZIP	

☐ **Credit Card**   ☐ **Check / Money Order**

Credit Card Number	
Expiration Date	
Signature	

Please Mail to: Book Jungle
PO Box 2226
Champaign, IL 61825
or Fax to: 630-214-0564

ORDERING INFORMATION

web*: www.bookjungle.com*
email*: sales@bookjungle.com*
fax*: 630-214-0564*
mail*: Book Jungle PO Box 2226 Champaign, IL 61825*
or PayPal *to sales@bookjungle.com*

Please contact us for bulk discounts

DIRECT-ORDER TERMS

**20% Discount if You Order
Two or More Books**
Free Domestic Shipping!
Accepted: Master Card, Visa,
Discover, American Express

www.ingramcontent.com/pod-product-compliance
Lightning Source LLC
Chambersburg PA
CBHW081200170626
46813CB00009B/3267